I0824327

EARTH 7

ALSO BY DEB OLIN UNFERTH

Barn 8

Wait Till You See Me Dance

I, Parrot (with Elizabeth Haidle)

Revolution: The Year I Fell in Love and Went to Join the War

Vacation

Minor Robberies

EARTH 7

A Novel

Deb Olin Unferth

Graywolf Press

Published by Graywolf Press
212 Third Avenue North, Suite 485
Minneapolis, Minnesota 55401

www.graywolfpress.org

Published in the United States of America
Printed in Canada

ISBN 978-1-64445-394-0 (hardcover)
ISBN 978-1-64445-395-7 (ebook)

2 4 6 8 9 7 5 3 1
First Graywolf Printing, 2026

Library of Congress Cataloging-in-Publication Data

Names: Unferth, Deb Olin author
Title: Earth 7 : a novel / Deb Olin Unferth.
Other titles: Earth Seven
Description: Minneapolis, Minnesota : Graywolf Press, 2026.
Identifiers: LCCN 2025050006 (print) | LCCN 2025050007 (ebook) |
ISBN 9781644453940 hardcover | ISBN 9781644453957 ebook
Subjects: LCGFT: Fiction | Science fiction | Novels
Classification: LCC PS3621.N44 E27 2026 (print) | LCC PS3621.N44 (ebook)
LC record available at https://lccn.loc.gov/2025050006
LC ebook record available at https://lccn.loc.gov/2025050007

Jacket design: Vivian Lopez Rowe

Jacket art: Elizabeth Haidle and Paul David Mascot

For Lucy, Emily, and Elizabeth

I leave my skin behind. They are only cells.

—TANYA TAGAQ, *SPLIT TOOTH*

EARTH 7

1

Escape to Earth

1

In those years, the sky was full of sulfur and diamonds, shot into the air by cannons to scatter the sunlight. The population of Earth had been falling for decades, and the drop did not have a sole cause. And Rosemary was leaving. She was taking her child with her, of course. The child was five, had a grave face and a funny little march, and could have become anyone at that point, her mind still plastic and watery.

They said their goodbyes to the team. Dr. Das came in with a gift for the child, a cloth animal. No one could tell what it was supposed to be—a snake? Everyone assumed Rosemary was leaving to protect the child—from radiation or disease—and she let them think that, but really she was leaving because she was sick of people, had put up with them long enough, she felt, had certainly given them a fair chance. There were fewer people, yes, but still too many, too close together, and she'd had it.

She and the child got on the company bus and rode it to the coast. They slept on a ship, ferried below in a submarine. Two days of travel. At last they sank into a circle of glowing pods.

Rosemary pointed at one of the orbs. "That's ours."

A few sea trees, a hulking nuclear generator. Some leftover construction equipment. The child clutched the cloth animal.

"Can we go back up now?"

"Not yet."

They gathered their things. They walked through the decompression chamber and entered the pod.

Years went by.

2

The child marching back and forth across the pod, the swoosh of her pants.

Soft chatter. Over dinner. At lesson time on her device. Rosemary on the far side of the pod at her workstation.

The child in her safari greens, sitting on the rug, zooming through screens with her finger, talking to herself, something about insects. Or constructing a school assignment with paper and paste, singing. Or pressing a button to lower the shades, pressing it again to raise them.

A message from Rosemary's colleague Dr. Das. *Have a look at my notes. I'm not sure I get what you're doing here.*

The child trying to squeeze her stuffed snake into the grower, narrating a story about a snake and a lettuce conversing. "Will you be my friend?" the snake said solemnly.

A bit smaller than Rosemary would like. Efficient cubes and rectangles—beds, tables, chairs. A slightly antiseptic smell, not so different from the lab. Windows all the way around, the sea lit up by blazing flood lamps. A dozen machines humming.

The bright banner, *Welcome to Sea Garden*, came down pretty quickly. A vase of fake flowers also disappeared. A serviceperson came by wearing a company cap low enough that you couldn't see his eyes. He tested the generator, waggled his fingers at the child, called out two incomprehensible syllables, floated off.

White sounds: The nuclear generator churning from cycle to cycle. The grower spraying at intervals. Any shifting of their bodies. The air blowing through. Lights clicking on and off. The glug of water outside. A rumbling in the distance—the other pods. Rosemary listened. In the early days, she figured the sounds would soon fade from her awareness, but they never quite did, and became distracting.

The child cutting with her safety scissors. "But I hate it here," she explained.

Tantrums.

Sleep.

Staring.

Water.

Rosemary giving her extra lessons because the schooling she was getting was pitiful.

In the next stage, Rosemary signed the child up for excursions, though they were a hassle and expensive. The child began leaving on a schedule. Monthly school field trips, five nights each. "Socialization." "Community." For the first time, Rosemary was alone in the pod for a few days and felt relieved—now she could *work*! She opened all her files at once and sank into them. She had what she thought of as her day work and her night work. But on the third day she felt an odd pain. *Yearning for child*, she noted. See that? People thought she wasn't normal, yet here she was, normal enough. She got up from her workstation and went to the window. Water, she thought. The child came back from the trips different, full of chatter, zipping around the room, running in circles, tossing pillows into the air. It took days to get her back to herself and then she slept as if ill.

No, Rosemary was not interested in Sea Garden socials, holiday parties, or game nights. Even discussing them was oppressive.

Could the child go alone?

Of course not. How was she supposed to get there? Walk through water? Rosemary had not opted for a corridor between the pods, as others had, and no, she was not going to have one built, and no, it was too costly to get a vehicle to come to pick up only her and bring her back. Besides, the child didn't need sweets and colored plastic. Rosemary refused all invitations.

She reached in and reversed a line of code, studied it, reversed it again with a small alteration, until the child interrupted with a chirp.

Did she silence her daughter a bit too much? Maybe. Rosemary trained her to wear headphones, to talk so softly that the sound occurred only in her own head. The child screamed but after a while obeyed, grew silent, words lining up and going by in her mind. Rosemary could look at her and almost see the thoughts moving through, her mouth twitching but staying shut. Rosemary rewarded her with talking sessions.

When the child went to sleep, Rosemary closed down her day work (on DNA) and opened up her night work (on consciousness) from its hidden digital vault. Hours passed—Earth hours, was how she'd begun to think of them.

But wasn't she *on* Earth?

Yes, but if she turned off her screen and hovered her fingers above the keypad, it was as if she were lodged in a dark void, underwater tides, infinity, rolling by out there. She focused better than ever, her mind widening, connections clicking together, vast strings of them across her brainscape, lines of letters and numbers. She could barely feel her feet held to the floor by gravity. She could almost feel herself release, unhook, from her own body, loosen from Earth (that was it, she could use that), as she worked and worked and worked. The transfer of consciousness, was it possible?

Several crucial breakthroughs for Rosemary during this stage. She knew she could do even more in the right conditions. She tried to isolate each sound, track it down, see if it could become yet quieter. Could this be muffled or turned off? Each watt of light from a machine: Could it be dimmed or darkened? Could she cover it with a piece of black electrical tape? In this way she made the pod less and less human, more what it could be—ocean or outer space.

Sometimes while the child slept, she lay down on the tiles and felt the hum of the pod. She forgot nearly everything from above: people she'd known and their trivial, complex, difficult psychologies. Theories that were so human rooted as to be useless. She thought about things that contained the properties of acceleration: suns and other galaxy bodies. Human creations: rocket thrusters, kites. If the child woke, she was frightened. Rosemary would get to her feet, turn the nightlights back on, and sing her a song about a bus, its wheels on a circular journey.

This was the stage in Rosemary's life when the night work took over. Human time began to lose meaning. Numbers became artificial, names theatrical, stillness a fiction. Once she understood these as illusions, she couldn't go back to pretending. She'd always been this way a little, but it grew more pronounced in the pod.

The child, meanwhile, enjoyed time segments (birthdays, mornings, dinnertime), she wanted "friends," found names convenient, went by one on field trips.

And she wanted to leave the pod. It was frustrating.

Outside, the sea trees broke into pieces and floated away. The sand on the shelf went by in surges. Some of the pods were being renovated, more corridors added between them. Noisy construction. Several pods emptied, residents left. A dozen pods darkened. A dozen more. Rosemary preferred it that way.

The child waited at the windows day and night. She said she didn't want to miss the fish when they came. Later—when it was clear no fish were coming—she just liked to stand there, she said. And no, she didn't want a talking session about it.

The child went on fewer and fewer field trips and then stopped altogether. (Why? Rosemary had been told, but couldn't recall.) The child was in the pod all the time now, pacing or lying on the floor, jiggling her knee. She had developed an outrageous habit of tapping her fingers against the window, drumming.

Possible side project: Put the child in stasis—?

What did you just say?

All right, no.

But sometimes the two of them sat side by side on the rug, talking.

Then she was no longer a floor child. One way you could see she was growing up. She sat on a chair or folded herself onto the sofa, a calf hanging over the armrest. She rested her arms on the counter. She liked raised surfaces. (And did she spend more time standing or was she just taller?) The floor stopped existing as a play space. Rosemary considered how the child would never see the floor in the same way again. The floor would mostly disappear to her. Rosemary integrated this into her understanding of space and matter. The world vanishes piece by piece, she thought. Either because it is too much in view or not enough.

A new, ferocious variety of tantrum emerged that slayed Rosemary. Wild expressions of despair shouted across the pod. The child hated "living in a vat at the bottom of the fucking ocean!" and said, "Fish are lucky to be extinct!" Rosemary lifted her fingers from the trackpad long enough to explain that she knew very well they didn't live at the bottom of the ocean. They were on a shelf was all. There were certainly farther depths. "I doubt it!" Screamed. But there were opportunities here—school, entertainment. This whole pod could be hers when she turned twenty-one. "I'd rather die!" It could be a solution.

A little while later, a closing observation, delivered coolly: "Only a very fucking cruel person would keep me here."

The sort of conversation they had.

Rosemary had a question for Dr. Das.

He wrote back, *What do I know about raising a child?*

You raised me, more or less.

Incorrect. I supervised your internship.

She repeated the question. Waited.

Bring her back and raise her yourself.

She repeated the question. Waited. Earth days and Earth days.

I'll consider it.

One more note from him the next day. *She'd need her inoculations.*

The child could no longer properly be called a child, Rosemary conceded. She was a "teen." In this stage, Rosemary recognized the utility of names. She knew names could be useful, of course, but she now experienced their convenience with such force that it felt like a revolutionary discovery. One word could encircle a jumble of ever-changing cells, could label it, even as it resisted definition. If the jumble had a name, you didn't need a definition. You didn't have to admit that you couldn't fully know or understand it. She must have given the child a name at birth, or at least a reference number, for the documents. (Rosemary herself had a name, after all.) What was it? She couldn't remember. What did they call her on the field trips? They'd needed a distinguishing marker for each child. (Had Rosemary gotten a little strange in the pod? The idea flickered and blinked out.) She considered, recalled. When the child was born she'd wanted a marker that expressed many points on an axis, many variables to be solved for. She had named the child XY.

"What kind of bonkers name is that?" the child demanded.

Well, who was she, then?

"Dylan, you idiot. People call me Dylan."

So the child had named herself. It was a terrible name. Might Rosemary call her XY?

"No!"

The child became Dylan.

Briefly, a betterment between them. Then a new, mysterious silence descended. It happened so gradually that at first Rosemary didn't notice.

Dylan staring through eight inches of acrylic, the exterior lamps blazing.

Rosemary sitting at her desk, consumed by the question of two minuscule pairings, how to shift their position so they'd be closer together in space and therefore time, how precisely she could read the effect. Day work: the reconstitution of life from twin helixes.

It was the most ordinary day of the decade for them. Twenty feet of purified air between them. Hundreds of miles of water rushing by.

There went that tapping. Dylan thrumming her fingers along the wall.

Rosemary sighing, saying it was morbid of her daughter to stand there like that. Why couldn't she stare at her screen like a normal person, instead of at nothing at all?

Dylan, not answering.

Could she at least turn off the exterior lamps? The lights were intolerable. They gave Rosemary a headache.

Dylan, not answering.

So, no, Rosemary didn't have the slightest inkling that anything was amiss, until the moment Dylan cried out, "Oh!" in a way that made Rosemary lift her head. There came a heavy sonic thud. The sand on the shelf rose in a tall wall, charged forward, and broke over the pod. Rosemary pushed back her chair and got up.

Outside was something that looked like a spaceship. A triangle of silver had landed on the sand. In her years underwater, she'd seen nothing like it. It must be an emergency. *The* emergency, she thought. A new wave of depopulation. Depop: the old way of thinking. The moment turned white. The sounds she no longer heard, the ones that had thinned away with time, though she thought she'd hung on to them, she heard them, they came roaring in.

3

Dylan Stein, lanky, slouched. In another life, she might have been a skateboarder. In another time she might have had bird tattoos, beaded barrettes, a handful of joints, been nodding along to a tune. Instead she had sat, stood, slumped, *waited* by those pod windows so long, her brain felt as if it had been buffeted by the force of the water, like the dead sea trees that had washed away over the years, or as if her brain had softened into a blob and dissolved, leaving behind an empty glow under a lamp, her mind.

In the early years, Dylan believed her mission was the fish. (Why else would she be there?) She was to sit quietly (which, honestly, humans had never been good at—that should have been a hint) and watch it all come back, roe by roe, not on screens from land, but from your own private underwater cabin, one thin layer separating you from the miracle. Because humans were *ready for solutions* (again)! She was learning all about it: extraction of nuclear waste one sea gallon at a time, deacidification by robot, flakes of iron sprinkled over the water like a giant aquarium, minerals shot into the sky, carbon plunged into the ground or piled up in blocks and strewn through the desert. Forget fishing forever. If the fish came back, people would love them fiercely this time—*peacefully*. The company had constructed the pods in the place most likely to see a recovery, where a faint ecosystem was hanging in there. Machinery lowered, trenches dug under water. Busy building for a decade. Deep-sea safari, shelf life. She would be there to witness the return, the revival, the arrival. Ocean, the original source of life and all that.

No, she understood by age eight that *she* was the subject of this experiment. The pod was not a viewing station but a vial of liquid nitrogen, a Nalgene tube. She was cryopreserved, vitrified, animated to imitate life. She was fed leaves that grew without soil, that smelled like poison. She was kept "alive" on protein that tasted like plastic, looked solid but had a slushy give to it when prodded.

She often imagined some new civilization generations from now, coming along to sightsee by the pods. They'd glide over on their nuclear membrane bus or whatnot and peer in at the Sea Garden residents, who'd be dead, frozen into their chairs, mouths hanging open. Or they'd still be alive, Dylan's descendants, doing something dumb like playing video games or fighting, holding war tournaments where they tore each other to pieces and regenerated. Perhaps they'd sell tickets.

For a few innocent years, she'd had the field trips. The children of Sea Garden were rounded up each month, herded onto a sub, and taken to see ancient shipwrecks, undetonated warheads, defunct fishing infrastructure, artificial reefs—the contents and contours of the shelf. She slept in a bunk, ate power snacks, told sea ghost stories. She was an explorer of the dead deep and the shallows. "Our mission is to find life," said Will, their trusty education guide. "Delicate, transient life." He wore an undersea outfit that had a bow tie printed onto it, part clown, part docent. "We wait and we search, not knowing how long it will take. I don't know about you, but I plan to be here to see it. Who's with me?" At which point thirty little hands shot up. Dylan's too. "Me, me, me!"

She had a shock of insight on a trip to see a graveyard. A thousand creatures the size of elephants, sea animals previously unknown, skeletons under spotlights that Will flicked on by remote. They'd congregated and all died together. This place was one of the last to be contaminated, Will said. They'd become sick and loped along as best they could until they arrived here, a holy site or birthplace, perhaps. One day scientists would study it, Will said. Build their careers on it. She stared out and understood. Nobody was waiting for any fucking fish. A new beginning was not on the way. The end had come and gone. She was part of the rubble.

The sub wheeled around and headed back to the pods. She sat, hands folded, the weight of leagues of water pressing down on her.

On the next trip, she led a class mutiny, demanded to go to shore. Turf expedition: amusement park, bonfire, camping, stars. She got the whole class to campaign for it, chanting and banging their lunch trays on the steel walls of the submarine like inmates. Their faces took on a frenzied, possessed gleam.

Gradually Sea Garden residents gave up on Sea Garden. No one wanted to be locked in a small transparent dome—except her mother. One by one, families packed and left to take their chances on the surface. Her comrades held goodbye parties she couldn't attend, and then they were lifting off the shelf. Pod after pod, going dark across the water, leaving her there. Her two best friends left, which was a blow. Sea Garden was transforming into something else: underwater desert island. Beachless, waterful, swimless. Meditation retreats, ecological seminars, avant-garde adventures. Ecotourists and researchers came and went. Stayed two weeks, three (because really it was claustrophobic down there), not *years*.

Dylan. Trapped under a glass bowl with her mother like a couple of aberrant insects. Saved but left to suffer.

Her mother. A woman so creepy she liked to turn off all the lights and lie on the floor as if they were in a coffin. Dylan got hysterical when she did that.

She could smell her mother anywhere in the pod. Her clothes, her hair, her food, which she picked leaf by leaf from the grower.

She could hear the groaning of machinery outside. She could hear the sea bumping against the pod, a rustling in the silence. Sometimes a nearby pod would light up and she knew there were tourists visiting but she had no way to reach them. A few weeks later, the pod would go dark.

She ran her fingers along the seams of the pod, tapped the walls and windows. They were made of an acrylic mix, four shades of one color. The furniture—was it made of the same material? Yes, but it had a sheen to it, neither transparent nor obscure. Indestructible, unlike the corridors between the other pods. She could see them out the window, corridors like flimsy tubes. They looked like tin, assembled on the cheap. They broke under the force of the water, detached, or just hung there. But the pods themselves were solid, would last until the end of time. Then you could shake them out and start again.

The only feral thing was the water.

Sometimes she could feel the pod swaying. She suspected its foundation had loosened and the sand on the shelf was working like tiny rollers, moving the pod, sliding it slowly toward the edge of the shelf, where it would slip off and fall to the depths with her inside.

Nothing to do but wait at the window. Each segment of water lit up as it twirled by. The sand mixed in made the water visible, full of tiny planes, fractions of illumination. She worked to see as far as she could—into the next stretch of water, and the next. Water raveling away, dragging its sediment with it. Motion all around her and inside her, too, as fluid swept through her body, as her cells died and were replaced, while she herself remained rooted.

Sometimes she was so bored, she'd panic, feel like she was choking. A few feet away, her mother would pick up her headphones, put them on. Dylan must have made a noise.

Come on, was it really that bad? Usually. But sometimes her mother did talk to her. Lecture. The great project. Life, artificial and otherwise. Her so-called preservation project: selecting animals, or rather subanimals, or their molecular representatives (DNA), and inserting them into cages, where they'd remain for all time. She hated her mother's voice, but since she spoke so little, Dylan listened. Sometimes her mother asked questions and Dylan answered. Sometimes it was almost like having a conversation, or at least witnessing one, or being witnessed imitating one.

She waited to die. While she waited, she grew. She played with her device, methodically completed her assignments (her screened-in AI classes limping along), filled out the additional homework from her mother (molecular models, devising and revising). She broke into her mother's computer from across the room, and found it shockingly dull. She got good at intercepting messages pinging around Earth. For a long time, she didn't interrupt or chime in. She listened and watched people around the world, living or describing living, or trading photos and videos of living. For a long time, she just looked at life surging—not dying. She began to make a plan.

So you're on a mission from Mars.

Yep.

Nice. You here to take over the planet?

You can keep your microwave.

I was hoping you'd break me out.

Nope.

That was an early exchange.

The message she'd chosen to respond to hadn't been secure, or that secure. It had been a question, a call. She'd listened. Not intended for her, but she'd answered and he'd answered and she'd answered. Behind his bravado, she detected a hint of curiosity, interest. She scouted out their ship with radar. It seemed to be more or less above them in the sky.

That's an absurd outfit.

Better than yours.

They were exchanging photos. His name was Zee. She didn't want to seem too excited.

You look human.

I am. I told you.

He had. He was a descendant of the original Mars settlements.

Why does your friend look like that? There was a person behind him. She zoomed in.

Who?

The face guy.

Oh. Genetic modification.

Mad science experiment gone wrong.

He's all right.

When are you coming to visit?

Her mother, racked to her desk, a glob of light in the dark on the other side of the room.

Where you been, stranger? Dylan rounded into a noodle over the keyboard, trying to keep the desperation out of her words, failing. She hadn't heard from him in a day. They were sending messages every few hours at that point.

Space walk around the ship. Hung upside down in the thermosphere. Replaced a spark plug.

We have robots to do that. Hoped she sounded too proud for manual labor. In fact the robots trundling around out there broke as much as they fixed.

You don't want to go out for a look around?

Oh, she did, she did.

She'd never left the pod on foot. Once, Will had suited them up in emergency oxygen harnesses, pressurized and weighted so they wouldn't bob to the top like floaties. He and the captain did a demonstration of walking on the ocean floor, moonwalking through the cabin making sea sounds. The whole class held hands and repeated aloud the steps in unison. Together they took a few hesitant paces across the floor, legs scissoring through imaginary water. "We look like astronauts!" Will called out. "Who wants to go to Mars?" The class tried to raise their hands in their heavy suits.

Another family left, including the kid who had once been the class bully. She watched the pod go dark. If it kept going like this, she and her mother would be the only ones left.

What's it like up there?

Not as good as you think. Cold. Dark. Everyone lives underground.

Not Mars. Earth.

I haven't seen it.

Why are you stuck in that spaceship?

Waiting my turn. Soon. Next, I hope.

Come get me. We'll go together.

Laughing sounds. *Why do you have to stay in that container? Are you a criminal?*

I'm a hostage.

Laughing sounds.

Save me.

Laughing sounds. *Quit complaining. All Martians live that way.*

She was terrified of losing his attention. Chat about trash, sky trash, ocean trash, how they were all trash, universe debris, everything is debris, recyclables, renewables. Chat about gaming, sex, Mars sex (he referred her to a learning module). Chat about food, protein, dust, the birth of microbes, animals becoming animals from a strand so small . . . , strand error, machine error . . . The more she wrote, the more he wrote. Sometimes they programmed dots to flow to each other at night while they slept.

Tell me more about your mission, Martian.

We're a salvage crew.

What do you salve?

Traces.

She didn't know what those were.

Traces of what?

Earth.

She thought of sand moving through water, fragments, evidences of Earth, elements glinting by.

Find anything interesting?

Not much left.

"I can't just live here forever," she told her mother. "I can't never see Earth again."

"That is so dull." Her mother waved her fork. "There's so much that humans never saw again. Everything." She took a bite of protein. "Anyway, this *is* Earth."

He told stories too. They scrolled up the screen and into Dylan's headphones, flying by. His own adventures, his lost moments, the search. They'd hovered in the dark for months, he said, coasting in the exosphere. At last the ship had dropped down through Earth's tight band of layers, slid straight into lower orbit. A blue shimmer.

What was it like?

Light, he said. *Mars doesn't have this.*

It's dark down here too.

Light, they rhapsodized. How all life grew from it. How all beings turned toward it.

Earth, they said. *Home.* Where their biomes belonged. *Boots on Earth*, they said. *When?*

He spent his days organizing traces others had collected. The traces were headed to Mars on cargo ships. He had to impress his superiors to get to the surface. He was working on it.

She had an idea.

I can get you Earth traces I know you don't have.

Of what?

She broke into her mother's computer with such practiced stealth and ease, she didn't even bother to wait for her to be busy with her bizarre leaf meditations over by the grower. Trickier was stealing a file. Dylan was bold, didn't care. She riffled through the files, searching for the one she wanted. Her mother didn't even look up. She found it. A list of DNA in her mother's preservation project, thousands of species long. Earth, humanless, abundant. She told him about it. What we're missing out on. The traces your superiors will love. Let's climb out of these storage containers—traces rejoining traces—and return to where we belong.

She sent it.

You have these?

Yes. (Okay, well, she almost had them.) *Are you coming?*

He didn't answer.

Not that day, or the next. She sent him long, rambling voice memos. He didn't answer. She was dying, she was sinking (she'd lost him!). Air, water, plastic, time, she was trapped within them, enclosed and suffocating. She waited at the window, pressed the acrylic, tapped it to hurry the pod's slow tip off the shelf to the depths—so slow it could take years, her unrolling like a cinch, decades to go.

On the third day, they came.

A rush of air in the water. A whirl of bubbles cutting through the dark, exploding. A bubble of bubbles bursting. Air from elsewhere arriving. Proof of elsewhere. A sound that wasn't even a sound but a pulse. Noise as a form of motion. A galaxy of light. An elevator of light lowering and lifting and leaving behind a craft, triangular and vibrating. Dylan's brain, running on static for so long, popped open, began glinting across quadrants. Her inner fan whirred to life, blowing away the sand and debris to accumulate in a dense pile elsewhere. She guessed even before she could see them that the miracle had occurred. *He's here. Zee is here.* Two figures stepped out. One word rose between her ribs: "escape."

It took them ages to crabwalk across the shelf, an eternity to reach the pod. Sand swirled around them in clouds. They looked heavy and weightless at once, like astronauts or insects, incandescent in the light. An excruciating pause as they stood outside the pod. She was barely aware of her mother standing beside her, but when the bong came, her arm shot out toward her mother because she did not know that sound, and in the pod there were no sounds she did not know. Then she remembered.

"It's the doorbell," she whispered.

"No," said her mother.

They did have a doorbell. It was affixed to the outside. She'd read about it in the manual years before, and her mother had laughed and said, "What adorable designer thought *that* would be adorable?" It had never rung. Visitors did not come walking through the water like futuristic robots. Company submarines attached to the side of the pod and people strolled through the decompression chamber like getting off an airplane.

"It must be an emergency," her mother said, her voice strangled.

"It's an emergency," Dylan agreed.

Her mother touched the control screen and activated the decompression chamber.

Suction, blowing air, the vibration of the hatch's motor, an increase in ions, electricity leaping through molecules. The figures entered the chamber. They had on helmets so thick you could barely see their features. Water lowered around their necks, shoulders, knees, while her mother watched, mesmerized. Dylan flew into the bathroom and got her go bag. She grabbed food bars, three cans of water. She pulled on what she thought of as her outer space outfit.

Wait, how was she going to get to their spaceship? Walk through water in a vinyl pantsuit?

No, she'd need special equipment. They probably brought extra.

Did it look like it?

No. Zee would figure it out.

Yeah? Did she see Zee in there?

Her head snapped up.

On the other side of the window, the Martians were pulling off their helmets. They were removing what looked like armor, what looked like crystals. They had odd mannerisms, acrobatic gestures, marching-band spines. Her mother was saying into the speaker, "Identify yourselves. What's happened? We don't have room to take in others." Which one was Zee? The two Martians looked alike, both a bit like Zee, but neither was Zee. Where the fuck was Zee?

Dylan took a deep breath. Delete. Begin again.

She stepped forward. "Open the door, Mother. It's the Martians. I'm going with them."

Her mother turned from the screen and took in Dylan's outfit. "Oh, is that all?" She laughed.

It unraveled pretty quickly after that. The Martians tossed a wet pile of equipment onto the floor, seawater running over the tiles. They got out some instruments and began waving them around. The space was so small, they could hardly maneuver. Their gloves involved a tremendous number of clips. The one who seemed to be in charge pulled the band off his head and shook out a long stream of hair. Certainly not Zee. They approached the window. Up close, their faces were as symmetrical as simulations and exactly the same shade. Dylan felt again that deep surety that she was in a zoo, that she herself was the main attraction.

"Greetings, relation Dylan Stein," the leader said. "The dimensions of this space. The traces could not be here." He held up a device and she saw: The list she'd sent was on his screen.

Her mother squinted at the device. "Oh, that's funny."

The Martians shifted thirty degrees to study her mother. Zoo. Other main feature.

Her mother crossed her arms. War games. Combat. "Obviously we don't have the infrastructure to support that kind of technology," she said. "That list is aspirational."

The Martians swayed on the screen.

Dylan sheathed in vinyl. Her mother turned on her. "And you. You have no antibodies. You'd be dead in six months."

"I can do the treatments," Dylan protested. "I can build antibodies."

"That takes two years." She added, "As you know."

Her mother's computer dinged off messages and notifications like warnings in an extinct language.

Earth. Dylan reached for it in her mind. A place of mountains and plains, where air moved at its own pace, unfiltered, unguided, untamed by humans, containing its own perfect mix of motes and water and all the rays of the electromagnetic spectrum.

Where was fucking Zee?

"There's nothing here," said a Martian, holding up an instrument. He shut his instrument. "Well, this has been fun."

"Wait," she said, "Take me." but they didn't seem to hear.

She watched them suction themselves in with vacuum seals, refasten their boots. They hefted their air tanks, weights, helmets. They waited in the bubbly midst of rising water. Her mother pressed the button to open the hatch. They walked across the shelf to their vehicle. They got in and left.

4

But she did get away. Not on that day but another. That's how these things work. You buck and buck, and then, with your weakest, most exhausted kick, the gate swings open. Why did it open now and not before? (Was it unlocked all along?) No matter, you escaped. It doesn't usually solve much. But you don't know that yet. All you know is that your mother changed her mind. "This was already the plan," she says, though you don't believe it. One day she signs you up for antibody treatments. An eighteen-month course. Immunities assembling, marching through the bloodstream into all corners of your body, your extremities, your large, pulsing organs. You are sick for days after each treatment. You begin life-skills training, another six months, lessons on money, contaminants, customs. You pack a suitcase for a year-long internship on the surface, after which you and your mother will "see," which to her means whatever she thinks it means and to you means you'll never return to the pod again.

Accept the gift she gives you: a small blue compass that you will carry for the rest of your life. Accept that where you are headed is your mother's place of employment. Not quite the clean exit you dreamed of, but solidly above sea level. Let her go with you as far as the transit station. Hug like a pair of damaged wooden puppets. Leave her there. Follow a line of people onto the submarine that will glide you slowly to the surface. Quietly credit the Martian, whom you haven't heard from since.

Just like that, you are free. Sort of.

Well.

The ascent. Not quite the rousing triumph she'd imagined—but whatever is? Dylan had not been in a moving vehicle since she was ten. When the submarine lifted, she was immediately dizzy and sick, gripping the sides of her seat. She could smell the other passengers, could smell her own body, her odor changing into something acrid and repellent. Her ears roaring, her internal warning signals flashing, she barely managed the accommodating half smile she determined to affix to her face. She clenched on the grin and felt it twisting into a grimace. She understood: No one stayed on the shelf as long as she had. That particular experiment ended years ago. The other passengers—ecotourists sipping drinks—had been below for only a few weeks. She was a freak. An attendant came through and asked how she was "holding up." He reached over and guided her seat back, gave her some eyeshades, ordered her to "chew these sticks" and "relax." He pulled a screen down around her that left her alone, gasping in the dark, uncertain how to get out without banging her way and creating a scene, gnawing on the sticks that were like a stiff cardboard that would not give up and go soft, until, either from a drug in the sticks or sheer exhaustion, she fell into a sort of static hold, while every sound battered her. At last the attendant came back and unfolded her out of the cage. ("Have a good nap?" he said cheerily.) She stumbled to the bathroom to vomit. She walked back to her seat, wiping her mouth, the other passengers eyeing her. She sucked down the cup of juice the attendant placed before her. "Halfway there," he chirped, which meant they were not "almost there," as Dylan had assumed (why else had he gotten Dylan out?), but also that she was halfway away from the pod, halfway to the surface, alive.

When the cap popped open to courteous cabin applause, she breathed in unfiltered air, unmechanized light. She coughed and squinted. The attendant urged her up the ladder: "Let's go. It's a beautiful day. Everybody's getting off," and it was true—there they went, climbing, stepping out onto whatever was up there. A steel platform on the ocean. It seemed to be passenger tradition to go out for a look around as soon as you arrived. But Dylan was blinded and couldn't breathe, began to panic, had to be helped back to her seat like a rigid doll. The attendants kidded her, though kindly. When she said she'd forgo the tradition, they smiled. "Tradition? No, my dear, the passenger ship is here. You're getting on it. Gather your things."

So, not the ascendancy she'd planned for all these years: Dylan Stein, rising from the water, striding onto land, leaving the sea. She was emerging from the depths a sea monster and would have to calibrate to human bit by bit. They got her out of her seat and transferred her to the ship in a breathing mask and goggles.

That night, while the passengers slept and floated toward shore, a new attendant guided her out to the deck. A vast emptiness of air swept by her—wind. The light still felt bright, but less so, and at least wasn't coming at you from all directions like "day." Dylan went out again by herself at dawn. She walked the length of the railing. Water, and she herself cutting through it. There was so much she could not control—temperature, pressure, light. But she could see *distance*, space just going and going. Horizontalness.

When they arrived at the shore, she walked down the gangplank unassisted. She climbed into the company vehicle they sent for her and rode away, sealed inside the vehicle pod (was how she thought of it). Hundreds of miles of scrub and trash. She watched out the window. She had never been so alone. She felt like she could go on.

She arrived at the place she had left as a child, a molecular collections lab in the desert. She had a few hazy memories (blinding sky, blowing sand, figures moving down hallways). The vehicle drove through the gate and stopped. A large industrial building. Cubes and rectangles blasted so white, they looked like they had dropped out of the sky. Exactly the kind of sterile place her mother preferred (why?). She got out, uncrunched herself from the vehicle like a broken origami, shrank from the handful of people who came out waving their hands and swearing disbelief at her size (though it would have been a lot more unbelievable if she had shown up the same size as when she'd left). They put her in a room, a rectangular sliver in a warren of rectangular slivers that ran down a hallway in a building of hallways. She put her pack on the cot.

She dropped a tiny *hello? guess where I am* to Zee. She waited. Like every message she'd sent him, it bounced back.

She spent a week between the walls of her tiny quarters and still she felt unready to come out. The atmosphere, the unbearable light coming through the window, the affliction of sound from every direction—and worst of all, the *people*. Unpredictable, unmanageable, whizzing by her room in no discernible pattern, with their loud footsteps, their unceasing conversations, their sudden shouts that could signal hilarity or alarm. She felt safest locked in her room with her console, from which she sent strings of happy-face emojis to her mother, who surely was not fooled.

Would Dylan ever stop complaining? Was *nothing* up to her standards?

Well, she did enjoy her small private bathroom, so much like the one in her home pod. *Home pod.* How the researchers met eyes with one another when she said that, one of the few times she agreed to have a meal with them. She *had* to come out to eat, they wouldn't bring food to her after the first day. She had to navigate the crazy hallways that all looked alike. She became lost again and again. They sent someone to be her guide. She had never felt more awkward in her life than when she had to face down the beautiful man-doctor who showed up at her door and offered to escort her. She attempted to "make small talk," the absurdity of the phrase, like manufacturing a miniature version of the real item. That was enough motivation for her to learn the way. The cafeteria was another horror. A smattering of researchers, who all looked alike in their lab coats, despite being from different continents. They scattered around the tables in messy configurations, murmuring and laughing in sinister tones—were they talking about her? She tried to take her food and return to her room but was halted by a robot-cleaner who grabbed her tray and swallowed it up in its maw.

And she missed her mother, which meant she'd gone demented.

The people. She tried to hide her dismay at how off-putting she found them. Up close, the researchers, their skin and pores, their shiny foreheads. Their human mouths that could be disgusting in fourteen different ways. She tried not to let her horror show. ("That's just my face," she said. "I wasn't *recoiling*.") Her mother abhorred her own body, she knew. Her mother moved as little as possible, her body cracking, cementing, solidifying. Her mother ate nearly nothing compared to these people, who mashed crackers into their mouths, sucked drinks the colors of extinct tropical fish. Dylan wanted to be normal. In her room, she was sick with disgust and desire. When she masturbated she thought of sentient AI trapped in metal, herself rubbing against it.

She wondered if she'd made a terrible mistake. In her room she kept her headphones on to drown out all sound. She tried to access what had driven her to ascend. The dream. It was in there. She couldn't locate it. She lay on her cot and searched her inner hard drive.

She received a memo to meet Dr. Das in the lab. Dylan knew him as her mother's colleague who'd once given her a stuffed worm, the single official toy of her childhood, but of the man himself she recalled only a large hand coming toward her to pat her head and then shoo her away. She padded out of her room in search of the lab. She wandered the premises. The building was so large, it felt like a town. She strolled down a line of storage compartments, passed a courtyard of cactuses, walked through a greenhouse filled with leaves. She found the biosecurity area. She went through a series of checkpoints where panels in the wall examined her face, palms, voice, sent her through air lock after air lock until she arrived at a human clerk, who sprayed her with antiseptic and covered her in paper. He swiped her into the lab.

As the doors opened, the tiniest byte of memory lit up in her mind like a firefly: This particular chemical smell, she knew it. Subterranean memories shifted. This machine hum. This category of grate flooring. These shapes, colors, this light. She remembered her mother leading her through these doors. She remembered containers of a thousand chambers that lifted and lowered into smoke.

She stepped into the lab, a tremendous room two stories high, and there they were, the giant freezers and vats, rows and rows of them, the dull silver of her childhood. She wanted Earth, the teeming cosmos. But this? Why, of all the places she could have gone, was she in her mother's life-size dreamscape of techno-optimism, alloys, titanium, and dry ice? Even as a kid, she hadn't really believed in it.

She walked down the row the way the clerk pointed. Figures in hooded biosecurity suits turned, tilted, watched her. She arrived at the end. A man on a stool sat up from a microscope. "Ah, here we are," he said. He lowered his glasses. He was older than her mother, and already she could tell he was better practiced at being human, an unfair advantage. "Look, everyone. It's Dylan, our intern. Up from below. Our runaway pinball."

She must have looked puzzled, because he sighed. "Pinball. It's an old game, 2-D, pixelated." He put out his hand, "Dr. Das," and she shook it. "Of course, we don't have interns here," he went on. "Outdated, laborious, barbaric. What's wrong with learning the old-fashioned way, by module? But your mother insisted. So here you are. Can't say I'm thrilled. You'll start tomorrow."

"Tomorrow?" She looked around. "Will I work in my room?"

His eyebrows came together.

"Won't I get a disease?"

"You've had every vaccination." He tapped his screen. "You've had preventive immunotherapy."

But it was people she wanted to avoid, not what they carried.

Well, he was wrong about pinball. She knew what pinball was. It was 3-D, not 2-D. In fact, the original pinball was *real*. It was a *real* ball kept in a real box, and the ball was a mirror—if you held it up, you saw your own face. Players used mechanical arms to push it around a noisy, strobing box while they laughed. They won when they made it slide down a hole forever and it was gone. But he'd called her a "runaway pinball." Was such a pinball possible? A ball that jumped its lane, made a break for it, joined the last wild bison of the prairie? (There was a game that went like that.) Dylan had escaped the pod, made it to the surface, only to find herself in another pod, yes, but she had made it this far. Maybe there was more.

He leaned forward. "Come on. Be in the world. That's what you came up for, right?"

"I just . . . I didn't know it would be so loud."

"Ah." He brought his hands together in a deafening clap. "Welcome to Earth. Such as it is."

Anyway, she began her internship.

Boots on Earth, she wrote to Zee. It bounced back.

The internship consisted mostly of Dr. Das giving her lectures on topics so elemental, she'd learned them from her mother by age eight.

"Let me tell you about our research, Dylan."

She tried to be game. "Oh, is that what you're doing?"

He gestured to the line of cryochambers. "Our molecular collection. You can think of it as an Earth backup." He winked. "You lose it, you break it, you have an extra."

"Convenient."

She knew about molecular collections. They used to be all over the place. Some were vast heaps of DNA, a thousand animals and trees. Some had only a handful of species, the essentials. Some were private stores—the rich keeping their favorite few in Nalgene vials in bunkers, their pet projects, their own dark visions of the future. And there were the civic-minded. They compiled what they could in small containers and sent them into outer space, last-ditch efforts to save the miracle. Less useful were the genome sequences—not DNA, more like instructions, how to make your own goat. Those never worked that well, starting from scratch. Always some ingredient missing from the batter.

There was a plan for every contingency. If an asteroid broke the planet into a million pieces, if all living things drowned in some jealous god's flood, if heat, fire, nuclear war, there would be *more Earth* somewhere, at least a little bit.

"I know what you're thinking," her mother had said. "Sure, it's easy to look askance at people who spent their lives constructing these things instead of saving what we had and making a home we could all exist on in relative peace. But come on, what were the chances that would ever happen?" Her mother's team had built the biggest collection of all. Earth 2. And they made duplicates. Earths 3, 4, 5. They hid them all over the world, some pieces roving, mobile, others underground. Alas, looters found the collections and picked them off, one by one. They were lost, destroyed, contaminated, shot out of the sky like skeet and left to scatter. Some of the collection wound up on the black market and from there disappeared. "The golden age of DNA is long over," she'd said.

Before Dr. Das could go into any of that, Dylan said, "So this is Earth 6?"

"Ah, your mother told you." He patted one of the cryochambers.

She tried to care about the molecular collection but she found it irritating and absurd, all this so-called Earth-saving. Everywhere she looked, she saw her mother and her mission. Dylan thought she hid her disappointment, but within a month, Dr. Das politely took her out of the lab and moved her to supplies. Then out of supplies to admin. Then to repairs. To the greenhouse, to receiving. This went on and on, a carousel of supervisors and new tasks.

Dr. Das sighed. "Your mother was so self-sufficient."

This really pissed her off. She went into the storage closet and came back with a broom. "I'll go outside and sweep the sand, all right?"

Dr. Das opened a drawer and pulled out a ballcap, winged it over. "Just don't die. I promised your mother."

See Dylan out there, sweeping. Instead of using the immense education her mother had forced upon her, she was pushing the sand around. The sand pushed back. She pushed again. She knew the researchers were watching her out the window. What the hell is the intern doing now? She thinks she's going to clear away the sand? The lab was surrounded by eight-foot walls to keep the sand out, and still the place was full of sand. Half the continent was sand at this point. Deserts all over the world, growing, moving. Nothing you could do about it. But okay, sure, send the intern out to push the sand around. She pushed one way, the sand pushed another, and that is perhaps not so different from most jobs since the beginning of the world.

By the time she'd worn herself out, it was getting dark. The security flood lamps came on and the space lit up. It was so bright, she felt more like she was in the pod than ever. Light whited out the sky. It was as if she were the only one left in the universe. She walked to the gate and clicked out, dragging her broom. She traveled into the sand and kept walking. When she made it beyond the circle of lamps and concrete, she dropped her broom, lay on the ground, star-style, seeking stars in the semidarkness. She felt nothing until she felt Earth.

Maybe it was a revelation. She'd felt so little *anything* in her life (longing, rage, hope), but out in the elements, with only a protective wrapping of simple cloth, she felt herself part of Earth, moving with it, drifting in outer space.

After that, her job was mostly outside.

She settled in as a sort of lone groundskeeper, watching over an empty land, raking a horizon of dust and rocks, sweeping sand that returned with the gusts, and this was fine with her, because meanwhile her mind began to secretly expand.

Each day, before dawn, when the ozone concentration was lowest and the heat at its ebb, she left her room, got out her equipment, and carted it outside. She swept the ducts and doorways free of the creeping sand. She combed the perimeter with a rake, made patterns no one noticed and that were gone the next day. She studied the sky, that migratory expanse, noted down on her device its path. She felt herself growing in thought and strength as she walked longer, saw farther, found ways to be useful—took over the water receiving, supervised the repair robots, fixed their half-competent repairs, read the research Dr. Das uploaded into her box, thousands of pages of it (certainly coming from her mother, no way was Dr. Das reading all that), tried to be the model outcast, just so long as he didn't make her go back.

Why were humans obsessed with making everything alike? Uniformity was a human derangement. The pod had been essentially beige. In the desert, any handful of wild sand and stones contained hundreds of colors, thousands of shapes. Nothing was ever the same around her after she'd lived inside sameness for so long. Hour by hour no square of ground remained unchanged. It looked different, was different, the sand tinkling across it, the light shifting, the interplay between cause and effect and randomness. The scale of the natural world, too, how seemingly infinite it was in all directions, the number of items it contained, their endless variants, their ever-mutating properties. The present itself was ongoing, shuffling, molting, amending, dragging the past with it, shoving itself into the next time segment.

It was in this stage that Dylan Stein began her deep research, meaning she thought about sand. Its mutability. When dry, it moved like water. When wet, a solid. The motion of sand. Its small stirrings, such as sand avalanching into patterns. Its large advances, its great project of sweeping around Earth with the wind and tides. Its endgame, its deep settling at the bottom of the ocean, only to be thrown upward in great planetary disturbances.

Its individuality too. Billions of grains, each finding a separate path, containing secret ingredients. Granules running off her hand, rejoining their dune brothers.

Sand as a sign of transition. The desert was its Etch-a-Sketch. Motion, its first rule. It was its own giant organism, had its own plans. It stretched over vast distances. It made mountains, carved land. It was the raw material for every great design.

The continent succumbing to it, depop making room for it.

Meanwhile, those stupid cryochambers. Fussy, hyper-hygienic, prissy, untrustworthy, trafficking in bits and pieces. Salesmen. Ice cube trays. Ridiculous.

She strode across the sand, history and the future.

She tried to imagine her mother out there in the sand and could not, so she claimed the space as her own. She barely read the rambling messages her mother sent, and she wrote back desultorily, if at all. She felt the claustrophobia of her childhood stripping off in small pieces—shards. How long would it take to shed it completely?

She went into the lab and asked if she could borrow a microscope. She saw the researchers try to hide their smiles because they'd seen her out there making sandcastles. Even Dr. Das, she could see, smiled, because he himself had looked through a microscope at this sand, and what more could be said about it? Especially sand like this, beat up by the wind, dragged up and down Earth's layers five times since being shaved from its shale rock at the beginning of the world. But he took out a powerful microscope and announced, "Curiosity is the start of personhood," and let her take the scope back to her room.

She looked. Sand that had been dropped off here by glaciers. Sand that had rubbed into existence from rocks. Sand that had blown in from overseas. Sand carried over by rivers before they dried up where they stood. Sand trucked in from shores by humans with their big, bright ideas: dam-making, road-paving, building-building. All the sand was made up of different elements. And she found skeletons in it. Microscopic vertebrae and cartilage. Some grains were actually an entire animal desiccated and preserved. And she saw creatures between the grains of sand, too, colonies of them, hundreds of species that had left their rivers and lakes and landed here, flattened and dried out into flakes. She studied these tiny beings. She wet them to expand them and see more clearly. Some moved. Some were *alive*. Tardigrades, those micro-animals that could dry out, go dormant, stay in tun for decades, and pop back to life with a drop of water, crawl across the slide. But tardigrades in the desert? Not possible. But here they were. Life is everywhere.

I've got traces, Zee. Come see. She laughed at how annoyed he'd be if he showed up, only for her to hand him a bucketful of sand. Her message bounced back.

Meanwhile, afternoons she reported to Dr. Das. "Dylan," he'd say, "how's the sky out there today? Any sign of those gems falling to the ground?"

Or "Hand me that screwdriver, would you? This freezer is a piece of crap."

Or "How's your mother doing?"

Or a lecture. "Have a look at this DNA, Dylan." A microscope, a gesture. "Tell her what you're doing, Wilfred." Nudging another researcher standing there.

"Mammoths," the researcher said.

"They're making mammoths, Dylan," said Dr. Das.

"Handy," said Dylan.

"Really Asian elephants with their DNA edited to make them look like mammoths."

"Ah," said Dylan.

"We have one so far," said the researcher. "Next we will clone the original cell and make ten. Ten beautiful mammoths."

"Sort of mammoths. Tell her what you'll do then, Wilfred."

The researcher puffed up. "We will release them."

"Smart," said Dylan. "Especially considering their habitat has been gone since the Pleistocene."

"Be nice, Dylan. You have a park for them, right, Wilfred?"

"Oh, your pets," said Dylan.

"Sorry, Wilfred. She's a little feral."

Her year-long internship drew to a close. She asked to do another. Dr. Das agreed. The second year ended. She asked to do another. Dr. Das wavered. Whoever heard of a three-year internship? Besides, wasn't her mother expecting her back in the pod? Well, Dylan wasn't going back to the pod. She'd rather die. That, Dr. Das said, was a subject to take up with her mother. A million messages passed between her and her mother. Escalating rage and threats. She'd run off, disappear, and her mother would never see her again. At last Dr. Das walked over to her table in the cafeteria, knocked on it with a fist. “All right, you’re a groundskeeper.”

She was already basically a groundskeeper. She said so.

“Good. Just keep doing what you’re doing.” He pointed at her. “The research too.”

“It’s not research.”

“It is.”

“I’ll stop.”

“Your mother’s orders.”

So she stayed. She began receiving a (small) paycheck. She worked on her research. She swept back the sand at dawn.

5

"Mother," Dylan said carefully. The worst had happened. It had taken a long time, five years, but her mother had come. Dylan pulled out a chair and sat down.

Her mother nodded. "Nice to see you."

"You look well," Dylan said.

She did not look well. She looked skeletal, as if deflated, as if shrunk in water slowly. Why had she come? Dylan was worried.

The cafeteria was empty. She'd stayed clear of the fanfare when her mother arrived, and they'd agreed to meet here. Neutral territory, a roomscape of identical white squares hovering at different elevations: tables, chairs, floor. Lunch was still in the air, some casserole concoction made by robots and cleaned up by machine, leaving behind a thin toxic residue on all surfaces.

"Let's head over to the lab. I'm sure everyone's waiting." Dylan already had her hand on the back of the chair, was rising.

"There's plenty of time for that."

Dylan lowered herself back down.

"May I see your room?"

Dylan placed her hands on the table, fingers spread. She frowned down at them. "All right."

She meant to just crack open the door to her room, let her mother glance in, and quickly shut it, but the woman glided in and put her bag down on the floor. It was a terrible thing to have her mother in her room, eyes running over her belongings. The window was two feet across and stuck into the wall like a light beam. Dylan crossed her arms in front of it and waited.

"I'm a company employee, Mother. I'm a groundskeeper. I'm like a janitor."

"I know what you are."

"I live here now, is what I'm saying."

"I can see that."

"I'm not coming back to the pod."

What could Sea Garden even be like now? Water whistling through empty pods owned by wealthy madmen who saved them as bunkers.

"I understand."

"Just so that's clear."

"It is."

The visit began.

Two of them, instead of one, in the hallway, going to dinner. Dylan could feel the researchers part to let them go by in silence.

In the dark Dylan pulled on her work outfit. Her mother stood by the door. She wanted to come along. But Dylan didn't want her to come along. Her mother should stay here or go to the lab or meet with Dr. Das. Dylan was going outside, and she knew her mother didn't like to be outside.

Not so. Her mother enjoyed the outdoors.

Dylan let out a long breath. When had her mother ever, *ever*, "enjoyed the outdoors"? The work was boring, too, don't forget. Just sweeping sand, hauling sand. Her mother would be bored and Dylan *knew for a fact* that her mother hated to be bored. No, her mother said, she liked to be bored, and anyway she wouldn't be bored. And Dylan went into the bathroom and sat on the floor between the toilet and the sink for five full minutes with her head in her hands. On the other side of the wall, she could hear her mother breathing. Then she got up and took her mother outside.

Her mother watched her sweep the desert, watched her pull out her device and mark down a few notes, watched her check up on the robots that were destroying, with their incompetence, refrigerators, generators, windows, walls. Watched, *stared* at her from a chair, while Dylan napped. Days of this. Out in the sand, the wind pelted them with tiny stings. Nights, too, while Dylan slept on the floor on a mat, her mother on the cot (though Dr. Das had offered her mother a nicer room, in the better wing), she could feel her mother watch her in her sleep. She could feel her mother's dreams leaking from her brain into her own (a dream of cold emptiness, how depressing). Her mother was taking over her brain.

Mother and daughter, coming down the corridor in their getups, sitting at dinner, not saying a word, standing outside in the night like they were holding a séance.

"Are you thirsty?" Dylan said.

Silence. Standing in the sand.

Are you staying? Dylan didn't say.

Standing in the sand.

Zoom out. Colorless land, dim sky, gray water in the distance.

Occasionally there was talk.

"I wish you showed more interest in the preservation project."

"It's idiotic. All that equipment will fail."

"So do it better."

"Earth is done with all that, Mother."

Or her mother standing in front of the shelf in Dylan's room where Dylan had some models printed. "I see you're doing a sand study."

"I'm just playing around."

"You never played, not even when you were a child."

Dylan resisted the urge to step in and block the models. "They think it's a waste of time."

"Who?"

She gave a little wave. You know, the researchers, she said without saying.

"You don't know what they think. You don't know what they call it. What do you think? What do you call it?" Her mother touched the microscope. "And what is this?"

Dylan flinched, but a bit of tightness in her chest loosened. "Just looking at sand."

"I see."

She shifted. "I found some tardigrades alive in the sand out there," she let herself say.

"Show me."

The emergency loudspeaker gurgled to life, bleated out a series of tones, and fell silent. It did that every day.

"All right."

Another week went by. Still, her mother stayed—why? She searched for her mother's breath in the dark through softly blowing air.

Dylan slumped behind her mother when she went to visit the lab, waited while she examined the freezers and cryotubs. The researchers gathered around, deferred to her, while she sat in front of the monitor, silently outthinking everybody. Dr. Das clicked around the screen, showing her what they'd done, boasting.

"This mammoth project is a waste of time," she said. "Mutant mammoths. Not even mammoths. Can we get a little creative? This equipment will all fail. Is there another way to preserve molecular life? Now, that would be a project. Did you see what Dylan is doing?"

A dozen heads turned toward her. "What are you doing?" one said.

Dylan froze. "I'm not doing anything."

Was she here to stay? The idea was losing its edge. Was there something normal, or almost normal, about living with a relation? A rock flung at an earlier era?

"Listen, Mother, there's something I want to talk to you about." They were out in the sand. "It's time for you to get your own room."

Overhead, the satellites were clouded out here and there—rain? Couldn't be.

"You could stay on the same floor," Dylan went on. "We'd be right next to each other."

"I'll be gone in a few days," her mother said.

Dylan blinked. "What do you mean?"

"I'm leaving."

"But you're working."

"I'm observing."

Dylan was somehow devastated. "I thought you were staying."

"I don't know why you'd think that."

"Or you were trying to make me go back."

"I never said that."

"Then why did you come?"

"I wanted to see you."

"What do you see?"

"I can't know in this short time. All I see is a facade."

Dylan dared to say it. "So stay."

Her mother turned her face up to the satellites. "I've got work to do."

"Do it here."

"Can't."

"That makes no goddamn sense. I know your research."

"Not that research."

"It's all you've ever done," said Dylan. "Nothing you say makes any goddamn sense. Do whatever the fuck you want. I'm just living and dying. That's all I've got on the clock." She dropped the shovel onto the sand. "So you came to say goodbye."

After her mother left, Dylan walked into the desert over the pebbles and sand, farther than she'd ever gone. She stayed away three days, brought a kit, and camped out. When she got back to the research center, she logged in. She scrolled and saw messages from her mother. She didn't read them.

Zee, she wrote, *did you make it?* The message bounced back. That asshole. He'd probably been an AI all along. She stopped writing to him.

"Oh, she's coming back," said Dylan. "She just has some research to finish," she said to Dr. Das (who raised a hand, looked at the ceiling, began, "Your mother . . . ," and shook his head), because her mother *might* come back, she really might. She'd be back.

Dylan returned to work. She shoveled and raked and swept, slept fitfully through the afternoons, waited, a dull ache, worked on her tardigrade research at night, tardigrades that must have been in tun far longer than any discovered species of tardigrade, tardigrades waiting, biding (she herself, biding), but even that seemed useless now (who was she trying to impress, her mother?). So she looked through the microscope, though less and less, and thought about sand, though less and less, stopping but not quite, and she would have gone on that way, perhaps stopping altogether, except one day Dr. Das sent her a message. She was invited to a party, a birthday party, everyone wanted to wish her well. Dylan was touched that he remembered. *She* hadn't, but there it was on her device: She was twenty-five and had a "party" to face. Couldn't possibly be fun. But she put away her tools and went to the cafeteria. Dr. Das, a few researchers, and a cake with her name on it in three colors of icing. She took a sliver to be polite. She tolerated the photo of them all clustered uneasily together, she grimacing in the middle. Then a gift, handed to her in a card. She opened it. She wondered for a moment if they were making fun of her. But, studying their faces, she decided that, no, they meant it. They'd all discussed it, how sad it was that Dylan was so odd and all alone, and Dr. Das had gotten the company to pay for this "gift," or, worse, he had taken up a collection. Dylan was going to have to endure this. A two-week stay at an all-inclusive, fully terraformed resort that insisted on the name Vacationland for Singles. That's how little they know me, she thought of the only people who knew her, other than a madwoman and a missing Martian. They imagined she'd find this fun. Unbearable. Why hadn't they gotten her one of those VR packages where she could just stay in her room and log in if she felt like it? Her face must have flashed the truth before she quickly arranged her features, because a researcher she didn't even recognize bleated, "We know you like the beach . . ." and trailed off.

Sand, she thought, I like sand.

"The woman likes sand," said Dr. Das. "The most beautiful

sand in the world lies on that beach." He patted her shoulder. "That's a vacation."

Dylan couldn't help it, she (almost) felt like smiling.

She packed a suitcase and got into the vehicle they sent for her. She arrived and settled in.

6

A Martian on a stony landscape. Loading broken toys into a cargo bin. One of the toys dropped, a small stuffed turtle. It rolled over twice and stopped. The Martian grinned. Gravity.

2

She, Robot

7

Who's the new girl and why does she love the robot? Is the new girl the type who always gets the joke and has a rejoinder that keeps the whole room laughing? Who plays tennis, has a dog who runs with her through the park? The type you'd want at your cookout? Who you'd root for?

No, she is not.

So why was she at Vacationland for Singles (terraform area .0469), far from her secret research lab, clearly making eyes at the robot?

She did not join in the fun on disco night or go jogging after flying objects on the beach with new friends. From the first day she was mooning up and down the sand alone and then stationing herself at the cantina to watch the robot click click click and serve drinks for hours, until it disappeared at dinner, likely going to its charging station, whereupon the girl would sulk back to her room, only to reappear in the morning, set herself up at the cantina with her device, and anxiously wait for the robot to arrive.

What a disaster, this girl—Dylan was her name. Even if it was an especially nice-looking robot.

Maybe that's what everyone was thinking. Maybe that's what Dylan herself was thinking—I'm such a loser, falling for a robot (though that's not what she was thinking)—but it didn't matter what they were thinking, because Melanie was not a robot and couldn't believe everyone thought she was. Partly it was the skin treatments. She'd had all the best ones since she was nine and it was true her skin had a metallic sheen—legacy of a life left behind.

She didn't try to convince them otherwise. She wore her professionalism like a suit. Let them believe whatever they liked. But Melanie was a woman of blood and guts and shit and water, and she'd never told them what she was or was not, because they had not asked. Guests dreamed it all up on their own and passed it on as new people arrived. She didn't care. Who would even want to be human anyway? But something in Melanie was snapping lately as she watched the guests dropping their towels onto the mat for her to retrieve, brushing sand off their abs, grabbing a power drink, and walking off, heads turned away, hands raised to friends cavorting in the waves. So when that skinny girl-dweeb, Dylan, came wandering up to the station, gawking like a boy, Melanie couldn't stop herself. "What, you like plastic?" and the girl actually said this: "Plastic is my second-favorite substance."

Melanie's assigned room was outside the reach of the terraform, a short walk beyond the barrier, in the utility building behind the washing machines, silent but for the machine hum. A few clothes hung on a rack. A mini-kitchen folded out of the wall. (She wasn't allowed to eat with the clients.) But there was a wide skylight, and if the garbage compactor wasn't on, the room was quiet, airy, and bright. Each dawn, she crossed the terraform barrier and was on the beach, her feet in the mystical water. It was a good job. She'd been lucky to get it. There were so few left. Really, a robot could do what she did.

She was back, asking for a lemon bubble. Melanie wasn't a robotmaid. "The machine works," she said, and turned away.

"Oh, I just thought—" the girl began, and stopped. She moved over to the machine and pressed the button, stood there meekly like a folded umbrella. She reminded Melanie of someone—who? Melanie's memory was trash. The girl raised her lemon bubble in an awkward mock cheers. Melanie melted a little. Cheersing a robot! Melanie wasn't a rock, you know. She laughed. After that, it went better.

"Why don't you enjoy the—" Melanie pointed with her chin to the water and the guests in the waves.

"I hate the ocean."

"People over there. You might get a date."

"I hate people. I don't want a date."

"I can get behind that."

The girl drained her drink. "I like sand." She turned and looked at the sand. "Not that I see any here."

"You're not making sense. But that's all right. That's sand right there."

"Not real sand."

"Realer than the rest of this place." Melanie tilted her head up. "Sky's not real."

The girl shrugged. "The food seems real."

"Do I seem real?" Melanie said, because she seemed like she might know. Melanie felt the girl's eyes on her arms, her breasts, her face.

"You're better than real," she said.

A deep truth about Melanie: She had a time bomb in her face. Several. Not the way all human faces are time bombs—the sinking, the sagging, the drying up, the dropping, the dying, and finally dead. No, her face had fiberglass implanted below the surface of her skin in such a way that it couldn't be removed, and that had exploded in 34 percent of individuals who'd been stupid enough to pay to have it put in. That wasn't the only piece of her vulnerable to spontaneous combustion. She had permanent alloys, acrylics, nanomaterials—filler implants that were almost as old as she was and that anchored onto disintegrating bone. The entire apparatus held up a fortress of other fillers. Each year you could see it all deflate a few hundredths of an inch. It would one day collapse. She held her body, especially her head, carefully, moved with economical right-angle precision.

The celebrity surgeon had always said, "Oh, you'll thank me for this later. I'm the best surgeon in the world. I'm earning the mug, the T-shirt. You'll be so grateful you didn't wind up on a stunt show." *Celebrity Plastics*, fifteen seasons. Melanie had been on seven of them, the most frequently recurring guest on the show. How the surgeon would laugh if she could see Melanie now, growing old alone, waiting on strangers, because what, according to the show, had been the point of all the surgeries and fiberglass and metals and treatments, if not love, or at least power?

Melanie had chosen this path and been chosen. Plucked by a producer out of one of the post-depop group homes where she'd lived with fifty other kids, sleeping on a mat in a row, life of a prisoner, child of the times. Promised food, fame, and so on, be a so-called star. Her first day, she'd walked into the softly lit studio: clean, classy, imitation wood running over the floor, a ceiling of painted sky, a forest of lights and silver mics. On the set, the celebrity surgeon herself was tossing her hair, posing in a pair of adorable glasses. "Plastic is the stuff of human ingenuity," she was saying, "of invention, of creativity. We built a civilization out of it, and you can build a self out of it. Make yourself new. Leave the past behind. That wasn't you anyway. A bunch of cells that died and were replaced and that you have no control over? With plastic, *you* decide who you are, what you are."

Melanie was spellbound. She knew she would do whatever the surgeon wanted.

Six seasons later, the world before the world of the show seemed so faded and degraded, she barely remembered it, and she batted it away when she did.

But then there was the incident with the beads.

"I don't know," said Melanie. Beads injected into her face? For the first time she had a bad feeling, a doubt. "Beads?" It just didn't sound right.

The celebrity surgeon uncocked her head, syringe aloft. "Melanie, do you know how lucky you are? Only a handful of injectors know how to use this material. I'm the top company injector." Really, that should have been a warning—if the *celebrity surgeon* was the top injector, how many injectors could there have been?

Later, when the company was "discontinuing use" of the beads, the surgeon herself brought the documents to her to sign—a legal "nonresponsibility" release, a posttreatment waiver, a nondisclosure agreement.

"Wait." Melanie didn't understand. She was in the recovery room, watching old episodes of *Celebrity Plastics* with the props assistant. She was trying to read the documents, which had words like "disfigurement" and "deformity," but the surgeon kept leaning over and sticking her finger on the screen, scrolling.

CELEBRITY SURGEON: Just pull up the signature box.

MELANIE: Shouldn't I read it?

CELEBRITY SURGEON [in gentle-explain voice]: Sure, if you want to read all that. [Finger, scrolling]

Later, it made so much sense.

The problems it could cause decades down the line. You put

that in your face and it's supposed to stay there fifty, seventy years—what do you think is going to happen? It couldn't be removed surgically (though the surgeon had initially said it could), because it was made up of thousands of little "nonabsorbable" beads that dispersed and migrated to different parts of your face. Each bead had a membrane that might pop, blow up at any moment. Even if you looked pretty good now—and you did, you better believe it—decades from now, there you'd be, in a nursing home, making eyes at the widow in the next wheelchair. Just as that cute old-people romance began to bloom and you thought you might have a reprieve from the slow drag downward (who knew that ego and desire lasted so, so long, longer even than your own *face*? But they do) and kapow, your face would burst and become "disfigured" and that would be the end of that. Not even the lonely widow would want that.

Melanie should have known. She'd been morbidly stupid and now the best she could hope for was that death would get her before the nonabsorbable beads did, and that the beads, thousands of them, would go into the grave with her, where they would be free to leak from their protective human shell at last, sink into the earth, contaminate it, a small sin compared to all the other contamination on the planet and beyond.

She'd signed the nonresponsibility documents. Of course she'd signed—and taken the payout. Then she'd walked out the door, not looked back.

From there it had been a long stumble down. She'd fallen apart for a while, drifted.

The last traditional filler she'd had—and she'd had plenty since *Celebrity Plastics* and the beads—was "medically experimental." She'd run through all her money, so she'd volunteered for a study, allowed a *new* new material to be injected, a different nanotechnology, made into a liquid. Really? Was that a good idea? Apparently. In her defense, she couldn't go natural at this stage. No free to be you and me for Melanie. The research, which she read feverishly online at night, scrolling and scrolling, warned that if you let anything get loose in there, the nonabsorbable beads could migrate, get stuck somewhere they weren't supposed to, explode. So you had to stay on top of it—lifts, neo-tech, whatever it took. Keep it all tucked in tight.

Besides, she'd begun to look slightly lopsided with all that heavy permanent filler.

A decade later, come to find out, *that* substance had never made it to market, due to complications: bits of aluminum spontaneously emerging, pushing their way out of 17 percent of faces, ripping the flesh, scarring, requiring multiple surgeries, unfathomable bills. So that was another potential problem area.

Her final procedure was the Regenerator. She had it installed in her face. It was going to solve all her problems. Yes, the accompanying brochure had actually said that, *It will solve all your problems*, and it seemed she'd believed it enough to go along. The Regenerator was a CRISPR technology, which was what people used to reconfigure the DNA of extinct animals, as if she were a *dead wolf.* It took apart the decaying DNA and replaced the rotted bits with new sequences. Each of her cells was running through the system, altering and refreshing like a screen. So in a sense she was a robot, or being turned into one, cell by cell.

She could feel the Regenerator in there. She could see its outline in certain lights. It gave a mechanical slant to her jaw. The Regenerator was a problem. She had to go back for follow-ups so the surgeons could study her *living cellular matter* and talk about her as if she were a slab of decomposing meat. They'd do an ultrasound *on her face*, knife open her chin for an adjustment, and then plaster it back together like papier-mâché.

Glimmers of insight hovered in the dark parts of her mind and acted the same way as a hazy dawn that you try not to wake and see. But daylight comes, no matter how tightly you close your eyes.

That was the end, finally. No more, ever again. Come what may.

She fell through the days. She felt herself sliding so far from human that humans didn't recognize her as one of their own. Meanwhile, around her, women were aging all over the place, in their skin, their muscles, their hair and bones, all of it fading, dying, decomposing in front of her eyes, and Melanie had to admit she found it beautiful. She regretted she wouldn't see her own natural disintegration. She got the job at Vacationland, held herself steady in all ways a self can be so held.

They were in bed, Melanie and the girl—Dylan was her name. Outside the window, the sun was beginning to rise. The tide was pulling the ocean up the sand over and over. How things had gone this far, Melanie didn't know. She didn't sleep with the guests, yet here she was, unclothed. Dylan had to know. No way she didn't know. But she kept not knowing. They'd been sleeping together for a week and still she didn't know.

Melanie got out of the bed and drew on her dress. She was conscious of her arms, her lips, her jaw.

"Stay," said Dylan.

Melanie tossed her hair (the celebrity surgeon rippling through her) and laughed. She put on her sandals.

Dylan reached out a hand. "I command you to stay. Does that work?"

"Not with this robot."

Dylan rolled over the covers, grinning.

"Walk with me," Melanie said. She picked up Dylan's ball of jeans and tossed them to her. Something fell out, dropped to the floor. Small and blue. Melanie reached down. A compass. She turned it over in her hand. She held it up.

"My mother's," said Dylan.

She didn't know what she was doing with this girl. She supposed she'd always been a little self-destructive. Or maybe it was the opposite. Maybe she'd always had a thimbleful of hope. Because you never knew. Surely there was a chance it would all stay where it was supposed to. She might make it to the grave with no explosive incidents. She might die like all animals, the way any normal human does. She might get lucky: cellular disintegration. Life, then death.

She put the compass on the nightstand and they walked down to the beach. The waves were folding, turning, lifting, revealing pink and orange tints. "I love you," Dylan said. And though nothing around Melanie was real—not the waves she was watching, not the muscles in her face, not the blue in the sky, which had a filmed hue projected onto it to mask the sulfur, not even the horizon, which was enhanced and colored, and though it didn't make sense for a robot to love, it was illogical—what could Melanie do? *Melanie* was real, or 98 percent real, and Dylan was real. So Melanie said (and to her surprise she meant it), "I love you too."

8

A memory.

A misty room. Melanie on painkillers and gas. The room seemed sunk in water, wavy and translucent, sparking. The doctors were talking about the Regenerator, what it was doing, the hold it had on her. She tried not to hear what they were saying, but her ears automatically turned up the volume, while her mind turned it back down.

"I don't know what you mean," the learning one was saying. There was always one learning and one teaching. "We've come a long way with genetics."

"We fiddle with a few traits," the teaching one allowed. He was moving the sonogram wand over her face. From a great distance she could feel the cold gel.

The learning one chuckled. "Preventing a thousand diseases—if you want to call that fiddling. We can control appearance, ability, inclination. There's no limit."

"Now, that's true. There is no limit." The teaching one had the bluest eyes she'd ever seen. He always wore a mask and a hair cover. She'd never glimpsed his face. When he spoke, the sound emerged from behind layers of protective material and blinking orbs of sea. "But we are unimaginative, predictable. We work within our own framework. We pace our own cage. We do no more than that." He raised the wand and peered at a screen Melanie couldn't see. "The human obsession with hierarchy. It's so dull."

"I happen to find it immensely interesting."

"We neglect to consider the truly valuable traits."

"Such as?"

"The bedrock traits. I mean the ones we share with all life."

The learning one came into her view for a moment, making an adjustment. His eyes were a woody brown. They twitched above his mask and roved over her, seeming not to see her.

"Let's take, for example," said the teaching one, "the simplest form of awareness. The ability to sense. To have an experience, however elemental. It must be one of the oldest traits of all. *That* is a trait I am interested in."

The learning one moved out of her vision. "I fail to see what's so interesting. Even microorganisms sense."

"Yes. Even single cells." The teaching one's head returned. Melanie felt his breath coming through the mask. "Think of it. Life, decaying, renewing, passing into and out of millions of configurations—taking part in the mighty force of existence on a longer time scale than we can imagine. Yet we piddly humans don't get to experience any of it. We get only this one time stamp, this moment, this workday, these few years." The head disappeared but the voice went on. "But consider this. What if we could *preserve* something in these molecules? The simplest trait. Having an experience. Perhaps that bedrock trait could be passed, unbroken, from form to form, transferred," he said. "Not at the mechanical level, as others have tried, but organically. That is what I attempted here."

"Doctor, am I understanding you? Are you saying there may be some form of eternal life here?"

"All matter has eternal life. I'm saying there may be something here that *experiences* it."

She blinked at a ceiling of beige.

"But, doctor, if all this is happening at the cellular level, how will you know if you succeeded?"

"I won't. But it will."

It, she understood, meant *her*.

The teaching one put down the wand. Melanie's eyes ticked along the periphery—her head was in a clamp. She glimpsed the knife. She winced.

"Wouldn't that be interesting," said the learning one, leaning over Melanie's face.

"Yes," said the teaching one. He stuck in the knife.

9

Meanwhile, Dylan knew. Of course she knew. She figured it all out the second day. Too late, she was already in love. She didn't care who was or wasn't a robot—because Dylan was not the kind of fun gal who threw a ball for a Lab or a poodle or a pit in the park. She wasn't the type to keep her friends laughing as they moved down the street in a showy pack. Those things required ease and comfort, which she lacked. No, she'd been raised in a pod in the ocean by a scientist mother who didn't know what to do with a child. Dylan had arrived on land with no ambitions but to be above sea level. She had not been on a search for love, she would have settled for normalcy, though it had not worked out that way.

She arrived at Vacationland on a small craft, carried her suitcase across the terraform barrier. Her mother had left, and she was alone.

Place was depressing, a collection of high-fashion people, all taller and cooler than she, dressed in absurd outfits that looked like life jackets, parachutes, biohazard smocks, based on some new idea of emergency hip. She tried to remain calm, stashed her belongings in her quarters, and walked down to the beach. The sand, she saw immediately, was unacceptable. Trucked in, of course, nourished, mismatched for the area, and mixed in with a glittery compound. Upgrade sand. Garbage sand. Fraud sand. She hated it and hated herself for being duped. And despite the brochure's protestations that Vacationland was terraform, not VR, she could see bits of VR everywhere, in the sky, on the waves. If you looked into the distance, you saw endless beach, but when you walked awhile, the sand became see-through, an illusion, a fake, an overlay video hiding rocks and trash. Who would want to walk that far? the company must have figured. No one. Vacationlanders were meant to stay on their mile and just look. She found this so irritating that she nearly left right then. She'd never make it through two weeks here. She walked over to the cantina for a soda.

Okay, yes, at first glance, she believed it—why wouldn't she? A guy was sitting at the bar. He introduced himself as "Blane" and pointed with his beer. "That's the robot." And, yes, there she was, a figure a little ways off, limbs moving with an angular stiffness, placing towels on chairs, head held rigidly aloft. "Amazing, right?" said Blane. Dylan nodded.

The robot brought over an orange drink with a company flag stuck in it. Leaned to place it in front of her. Her face sparkled as Dylan gazed into it, such a perfect set of human features, but also clearly an imitation. The robot stopped beside Dylan, swiveled onto one hip. "What, you like plastic?" she said slyly.

Dylan jumped. "Plastic," she replied solemnly, "is my second-favorite substance." (A lie.)

The robot gestured to the water. "Plenty of plastic in the ocean." She winked and strolled off, a robot with nothing to lose.

So she hadn't known in that first moment, though maybe she just wasn't letting herself see it. And it wasn't the skin, which Blane compared to a yoga mat. It wasn't the martial stride. Their conversation later that afternoon was quintessential-AI flirty, so it wasn't that. Still, that evening, while all the other Vacationlanders in the dining hall were collectively cooing over the last lobsters on the planet, Dylan looked out to the water and saw a figure in the dark and knew who it was. Her robot. She was already thinking that way. Her isolation and the robot's, joined. She'd been lost for so long. She rose, left the table, and went out, but the robot was gone.

The next day—her first full day in the terraformed space of .0469 Vacationland for Singles, where she had no reason to be, had never taken a vacation, had never had the desire to, had never thought of herself as "single," the very word implying the possibility of more than one, so not a word that applied to her, and where even the sand was a sham, a blend of ingredients artificial as Oreos—she went looking for the robot. She wasn't in the cantina, not by the spa, not in the restaurant. She found her removing bottled rainbow drinks from a compartment, chin held in that problematic way. Just a glimpse of her and Dylan's dread lessened. The robot dropped the lid with a thud. "No photos allowed over here."

"I wasn't, I didn't." Dylan held up her device innocently.

The robot clocked her head to the side.

"Is there any," Dylan swallowed, "sand around here?"

They were standing in sand.

"I mean, unnourished sand?"

She swiveled her weight to the other leg. "Maybe."

Ah, she was adorable. Dylan loved her already. Deep, passionate robot love. She couldn't say why.

She followed the robot. They walked along the water toward the terraform barrier and then through it.

A little while later, a few hundred steps outside terraform area .0469, Dylan was crouching, picking through the garbage, and scraping at the brown grit underneath with her fingernails, while the robot stood alongside her, waiting. She could hold absolutely still, Dylan noticed. It was the closest Dylan had managed to get to her, and she even smelled human, which was amazing. Something felt right. Dylan didn't know why she didn't connect with humans, but here she was calm. A robot. It made so much sense.

But her mind was already working, turning over the assortment of reasons this was wrong, a collision of them. Free will and AI. Ownership. Consent. Robot as company property. Image of a manic burglary attempt (she wanted to steal her?), herself imprisoned for robbery. Could she do it legally, buy her, rent (?) her? (She looked expensive.)

What could possibly be the matter with Dylan that she felt nothing for humans, but then a machine comes along and she's in love? She sat back on her heels, looked down the robot's long leg, ending in the most realistic artificial ankle she could imagine. Then she saw it.

One of the toes.

All the others were perfect—thin, smooth, sanded, painted into the loveliest little appendages. But the last one, the one nearest to Dylan, it was a bit . . . what was the word? "Canted"? It seemed somewhat large in proportion to the others—and bent. It leaned over the toe beside it. And was that a *blister*? The robot shifted, turned. Dylan sat back on the ground and stared up at her, her hair cascading down her back in ribbons of curls. But Dylan had seen it, and she knew. No designer would construct a toe that way. And this was not a manufacturing flaw. This was sheer organic imperfection. That toe, the smallest one, the toe of nicknames and songs, the littlest "piggie," the hero of the story of a wanderer who embarks on a quest, strays too far for its youth, and comes roaring down the road, crying out a syllable passed through generations, "Wee, wee, wee," seeking home, longing for it, racing toward it—*that* toe on *this* robot was real. And by real she meant human, because that is what this robot was.

Oh, Dylan. Oh, Melanie. You fakers both. You cannot hide every flaw. You cannot hide flaws that are not flaws but are mere signs that you are part of this world, a place where terrible and wonderful beauties are coming to pieces at every moment and others are constructing themselves out of the remains—a place, in other words, of flux, of history forever destroyed underfoot, forever rising anew from the ashes with the aid of air and water and physics and time. We exist in and as part of that destruction, that rebirth. In fact, *some* beings say the flaw is not of the flesh at all, but is instead the belief that you *can* isolate a "you" in this mad flicker. The idea that we think we can divide out and hold apart an unstable collection of atoms long enough to know it—*that* is the error. Some, such as a certain set of extraterrestrials (who do not appear in this story), see all mass as flowing together like uninterrupted light. They would say the flaw is that humans conceived of themselves as separate in the first place, that we imagined ourselves as privately taking up space. They would say the flaw is that we even thought up the word "flaw," as though there might be something wrong with the way we exist in space. Individuality, error—these, they reject.

Those ETs are still a long way away, but one day they will come and see this planet.

For Dylan, all else began to delete and update and slide into place. Of course. The voice, which was a tad scratchy. The eerie eyeballs that "darted" more realistically than those of any robot she'd seen, eyelids that fluttered, pupils that emitted emotion, *expressed*, though the skin around them was frozen. The hands, though smooth on one side, had more lines than necessary on the palms. The face—was it very slightly askew? Now that Dylan knew, she saw evidence everywhere, on her body, in her hair, in her movements, which suddenly seemed self-conscious and awkward. Her conversation, which yesterday Dylan had thought so brilliantly programmed, she now saw in it the delight, sadness, and fury of a full human.

Question: Was Dylan a virgin? No, she'd had a few uncomfortable encounters with staff at the lab. (Once, she'd set a pillow on fire with an old-fashioned candle, trying to be romantic. She distinctly recalled holding up the burned, soggy fluff, while the man, who found it hilarious, pulled on his pants, laughing. Horrible.) But she'd never been in love. Well, those days were over. Somehow it had happened. Dylan was falling in love, and the robot, who was not a robot, might be falling in love back, and that's all there was to it. It could be this simple, it could happen this fast. She saw this in the papery light of the unenhanced sunset outside the terraform.

But running alongside her happiness, galloping, was a thin and creeping dismay. It was as if a dark blanket had been thrown over the sun, or as if a false sun were fronting the real one. A dimness descended. This woman could desert her, she could not want her, she could die. She thought of her mother. Instead of empty joy, innocent and carefree, she felt grief.

She fell back onto her elbows in the sand, watched the woman (what was her name?) walk away toward the terraform barrier.

Back in her room, Dylan figured it out with a few keystrokes. Her name was Melanie.

Melanie, human and alone, like herself. Dylan wanted her. She paced the shag rug. She folded her hands over her face.

That night, while the Vacationlanders were playing a game that involved them lining up and marching in time to discordant music and descending backward under a stick that lowered and lowered while they all feigned (it must have been feigned) fun, Dylan came out of her room and circled widely around them. She headed out to the beach. She caught sight of her. A flicker of fluorescence in the dark. The possibility of knowing another human, of them knowing you back. Of discovering what was unknowable in each of you, and letting it be known.

Dylan approached, said hello. She reached for Melanie's hand, pulled her close. Melanie let her. Dylan kissed her, right there in the sand.

In that moment, Dylan could imagine it, the rest of her life, Dylan and the robot (Melanie) watching the sky, the real one—white and damaged and polluted—as Earth moved them in circles through outer space, decades going by.

She kissed the robot's face, her lips, her neck, put her hand in her thick, bountiful hair.

Days passed. Dylan managed not to let her know that she knew, because for some unknowable reason, Dylan sensed, Melanie did not want to be known. And this Dylan understood because she, too, had spent her life hidden. She kept up the robot charade like a pro. It was the greatest con job of her life, though she'd never conned anyone before. As long as Melanie didn't know she knew, Melanie would stay with her. That was all that mattered. That, and the fact that Dylan would have to leave.

Terraform area .0469, a pixelated blip of decoration hung over a landscape of human disorder. Two dots twinkling inside.

The day of her departure arrived. She paid for another week out of her savings. She was stunned at how expensive it was and felt a tug of guilt toward Dr. Das. She wrote him to say she was having such a great time! She was staying another week! She left her device on the bed and went back outside to look for Melanie. As the third week drew to a close, she looked askance at her financial situation. She didn't have enough for another week. Could she get hired at Vacationland? Impossible. She'd have to leave and go back to her (face it: basically janitorial) job. She'd never see Melanie again. Could Melanie come with her? Would she?

Blane hung his head in a pose that said he was disappointed to find he had to tell Dylan something she should already know. Dylan knew that look. She'd seen it before. They were sitting in a restaurant that changed gem-themed colors every four minutes. Opal, ruby, sapphire.

"Dylan, she's a robot."

Dylan dropped her head into her hands.

"Look, I get it," said Blane. "She really is so lifelike. Other than the skin, which is sort of like Saran Wrap. It's tempting. Humans are a pain in the ass. Unreliable, annoying. It can get ugly. Don't I know it! People change, you change, it's a mess. It's more practical to get a gadget. An investment too. Smart. Especially these days." He smiled grimly. "But listen, and here's where if you tell anyone I said this, I'll deny it." He lowered his voice. "To love a human, to fall for a human, there's nothing like it. It's risky, yes. But to risk is to hope, and without hope, well, we are done as a species." He waved in the general direction of the cantina and shook his head. "A robot . . . that is giving up. You're too young to give up. I can't let you do it."

Dylan glanced at Blane from under her hand. Emerald light fell over the room. She felt ridiculous. She felt like a clown. How much could she say? That the problem wasn't that Melanie was a robot, but that she wasn't? It wasn't Dylan's secret to give away.

She paid for two more nights. Then she decided to talk to her.

They were standing on Sweet Singles Street, terraform and VR swirling around them. The shops and spas and fountains flickered, shuffling into place when you looked at them, fading when you turned away. Melanie and Dylan were looking up into a sky that had a scene of angels blowing across it. She had tried to get her mother to stay and she had failed. She'd tried to befriend a Martian and she'd lost him too. Now she would try to get the woman she loved to come with her—would she?

"Leave with me," Dylan said. "Leave this place. Come home with me. I want you with me, always." She watched Melanie's lips. What would she say?

It could have been so romantic. But was it? Dylan had an uphill battle. Let's consider. This wasn't the story of two rock-and-roll misfits, two punk lovers wreaking havoc and taking off through the desert, smoke rising behind them. Dylan was, let's face it, a nerd, and not in a cool way—anxious in the extreme, monosyllabic around most humans, stunted. She'd known only lonely ocean and empty desert. She didn't have the spunk or vision of the legendary rebels, like Romeo and his babe. She was no John, no Yoko, no Clyde. Even Harold, even Maude, had something on these two. And this was not some Cinderella story or Robin Hood, where the poor get rich by hook, crook, or promise. This was no superhero story about beautiful people and bad fates turning good. This was no fairy tale, no one falls asleep and wakes to a new world, changed by another's kiss. She'd been part of no stories like that in any of her wanderings since she'd left the ocean shelf.

No, this was the story of Bubble Boy meets Plastic Girl. He falls in love with her, can't live without her. Plastic Girl is not young, wild, full of adventure, like the ancestral heroines of screens. Maybe she was those things once, long ago, but not now. But to Dylan the world looked cold and ugly without her. Melanie was magic. And Dylan was, too, when she was with her. She was whole. Dylan had been willing to accept the deal: live in the desert in a block of concrete and steel, sweep the sparkling sand, sit alone at night with a microscope and work on her end-of-the-world project, let that be where it finished for her. And she had been fine with that because she had no ambition, domestic or otherwise. Her one goal had been so elemental and achieved years ago: to leave the pod. But then she'd met Melanie, and now she wanted *more*. There wasn't a lot of room left on the planet for people like them. They needed to stick together. Dylan had hung around terraform area .0469 Vacationland for Singles for as long as she could, and now she had no choice but to bring Melanie back with her, because you don't walk off and leave the one bright person behind you. You do not do that. You have to try. Her chances were slim. She knew that. She knew she needed Melanie more than Melanie needed her, but Dylan was counting on need not being what drove her, but something less spiritless than need, something bigger. Desire, love, the Search. But how to convince her? She'd get down on one knee, she'd pull out a shoe, she'd detonate a bomb, raise a boom box overhead and play a song, if that was what Melanie wanted. She'd rev a car for a last fast chase across town, guns in the back seat, sirens and lights behind them, whatever it took, whatever she wanted. What did she want? Dylan stood there, hands hanging by her sides, atmosphere spinning overhead, wind tossing. What would make her come?

"Quit," she said. "I know, okay? I know. Just quit your job and come."

Melanie considered her from what seemed like a distance of miles. "What is it you think you know?"

Dylan reached out and tried to take her hand, but Melanie pulled it away.

"I know you're not a robot," said Dylan.

"I'm not a robot?" Melanie let out a bitter sound—a scoff or a gasp. "Oh, that's beautiful."

"Melanie."

She drew herself up. Her voice was acid. "Do not say my name." She turned and walked off.

Dylan thought of her mother, just a flash. "Wait," she called, but Melanie left her there in the terraform.

10

Melanie, alighting.

The first time she saw Vacationland, she came by air vehicle. She stepped down off the craft and emerged into Jell-O-colored clouds. She strolled along the misty yellow brick path at the entrance. She had a retro cardboard suitcase (made of plastic) and a fake letter of introduction on a device that she'd stolen, but she'd gotten here in one piece, barely, and on time. She liked what she saw—terraform sun and multicolored sea—even if she didn't like the work she'd have to do to stay. How long can I do this for? she wondered, turning her head up to the "sky" to watch the radiant angels commence a lively welcome parade, which they did for every arriving guest. She was not a guest but she hadn't yet learned where the service entrance was. The angels were breaking into constellations, stars were falling down around her like snow. Her interview was in an hour. This is going to be just fine, she thought.

Three years later, Melanie was standing in the same spot, the mist of Sweet Singles Street swirling around her legs. "I'm not a robot?" she said. She blinked. Dylan knew. Goddamnit. Knew all along. How stupid had Melanie been wishing she was? Melanie swallowed people like this. She ate them whole. But this time she was the one who'd been consumed. How had this happened? She was fine with being a robot. She preferred it. Not her idea, but she went with it. She didn't want love, that dull, faithless, capitalist trick. Not a robot? Of course she wasn't. Oh, to be a robot!

Shame swept through her. Disappointment. She'd really liked Dylan. (Why?) She shoved it down. Kept her robot face on, you better believe it. After the initial shock, she was more steady than ever. She stood in her ballerina-style slouch, the most human pose she had: a ballerina who damn well knew how to stand straight. For her, straight was a habit stronger than slouch, but slouch she would, out of defiance. Even her slouch looked like straight. Or, no, her slouch *was* straight, because that's how good she was, that's what she could do: cultivate a look that *suggests* but not *is* slouch.

But it arrived from the far-off reaches of her mind: She'd never been a ballerina, so even that level of her-ness was false, and she saw what Dylan must see, the levels of fake, the layers of plastics and acids, the lasers, the threads, the hormones, the glosses and wrappings, the lifts, the surgeries, the way her body was sustained on a pillow of products, and the Regenerator, which would preserve the whole apparatus for who knew how long. Maybe forever. A woman masquerading—why? The package she'd presented, the stratagems she'd put in place from her first day on *Celebrity Plastics*—a child and chosen—they fell away and she stood, revealed. But what was revealed? She'd been running for so long, she had no idea who she was.

And Dylan knew. Dylan was making a fool of her.

"Oh, that's beautiful," she said.

She thought of the celebrity surgeon, just a flash. Wondered if she was still alive, the hag.

"Melanie," said Dylan.

Her own name burned her. Melanie's fuck-you voice rose

between the iron columns inside her and came out in evil-robot voice. “Do not say my name.”

This girl will never see me again, Melanie vowed. She walked away.

She exited the consumer area and went back to her room. Outside the terraform, the sky had a silvery look. Bits of it looked blown out, sunken, smoky. Sulfur fell in flakes here and there, and accumulated on the concrete. She packed. She was leaving—not because of Dylan, fuck Dylan, but because she was through playing maid. She wasn’t going to do it, not for Dylan or anyone else. She was done. She folded her few dresses and skirts into her suitcase, snapped the clasp, peeked out to be sure no one—Dylan—was standing around out there waiting, because fuck her. Melanie was too old for this. Two bad choices, that’s what she had. Stay or go, and she’d given stay a try. Now it was time to go. She got on the company bus and rode out of there in darkness.

But there are always more than two choices, a voice in her head said.

She rode. She traveled back along the highways the company had taken over and blocked off. A tundra of clutter out the window. The abandoned equipment of abandoned human projects mixed in with the rocks and sand, the equipment of nature’s abandoned projects. The detritus of past worlds combed together. When the company bus reached the end of the line, she got off with her suitcase and waited on the highway, company lands all around, outlands in the distance, her last-ditch, past-life poverty rising to greet her. She got onto the next vehicle offered.

She passed into the transit area, a place of refugees and drifters, of people trying to get somewhere, of people trying to follow a plan, or who had given up on the plan, or who were still grasping for it but were stymied or stuck, caught in a snag, people moving like sand, pushed, gathered, thrown, washed out, people like grains of all kinds, each with their own makeup and history, the components of this planet, misplaced, cruising, would land somewhere. But Melanie knew where she was going.

She got on ride after ride, rode in vehicles so long of out fashion that they powered on modes of energy no longer in use and the drivers had to stop and buy more, black market, or even make it themselves on the side of the road while the passengers sat in the gravel and watched. She rode in vehicles so newfangled and experimental, they quit working after a few miles, and the passengers had to get out and help tug until they gave up and walked off.

She rode for three days, the holy number, the number of haikus and jokes and pigs, of denials and wisemen and bears, of the faces of certain gods. At last she arrived at the final outpost in the desert. Beyond, only sand. Earth was rotating into evening, sending gray shimmers shooting. She climbed down from the roof of the dune buggy, entered the opening in the wall, and came into a cluster of tents. Bedrolls and mattresses lay across the ground, some under a canopy of rugs, others in a row along the wall. Beyond these, just scatters of clothing. She stepped over the blankets, bodies turning in sleep.

An attendant strolled over. "Nice to have you back, Mel. Got cash or do you need an advance?"

"I'm just off a job, flush enough." She peeled off a few contraband bills, the old barter.

"All right then. That's your dump spot, sweets." He handed her a bedroll, pointed down the line. She walked to the end and sat down. A voice like a tail looping through: *Always more than two choices.* She locked up her suitcase and walked over to the bar, just a stand in the sand, whisps of people hanging around, no tests, no vac-passes, no masks. No particle-measuring devices. No infrared detector or otherwise. Just a messy clump of strangers hanging around, more crawling off their blankets, approaching, while the sun went where it was most appreciated—out of sight—and the heat wore itself out. Soon they were draped over their chairs, breathing into each other's faces, laughing, singing, calling out like this was 1999. Beautiful wrecked humanity, the also-rans, their infection rising and settling like a cloud, falling like drizzle over a contaminated desert.

She had run home. She had lived here as a runt after the second wave of depop, swerving between legs, chiming and dimming, before she'd been scooped up by the company, put into the home, and from there been chosen by the show. Still, she came back, again and again. Each time she failed, flubbed, fought, quit, ran, lost, came to pieces, she'd return here to gather the shards, humble herself. And here she was once again. Her, along with the usual yellow surprise of self-determination: to be "free of," to have shaken off the weight of, to be asking, again, Who am I? That quest, the original root of sadness and wildness. It had found her again.

But this time it felt different.

Over at the bar in the sand, there was a goblet going around, everyone putting their lips on the same rim. She took it and put it to her lips, daring their contagion if not their drunk. They were playing a game she hadn't played since she was eighteen and living with people she never saw again and didn't remember, not their names or their faces, only the particular way they called out their curses as they slapped their cards onto the table. Those people were gone now and these ones sat in their places. She put her elbows on the table and played.

She kept throwing fives that night—the winning number in this game: Right in the middle was where you wanted to be. She was so good that after a while people came over to watch. They'd never seen anyone play like her. She'd go far, this one. She was a warrior, a bandit, a sly cat, a star. Nobody thought she was a robot. They knew better, had known her, or her like, too long—but her playing made them speculate: What *else* might have been implanted? Was she so crafty that her cheating wasn't visible even to the sharks in attendance, or was she having an overdue run of good luck? Or could it be skill? Perhaps.

But it wasn't any of those, she could have told them. It was clarity. It was steadiness. She'd learned from the best, the celebrity surgeon herself, a woman who had no friends, who could make no bargains with lovers or gods, a lonely old bitch, but she had vision.

Melanie had never wanted to live forever. She'd never particularly wanted to live at all. But here she was. And when it was her turn to deal, she blinked and took the cards.

People have much bigger problems than yours. Yours is nothing, she told herself. Yours is in a future that may not exist. You might live forever? Crybaby. People have much deeper sorrows than that, sorrows they have to face, not imagine—accidents, failures, physical pain. People come down with weird illnesses that debilitate and sicken slowly. Loss is everywhere. Hers counted, sure. Every pain counts. She could feel it in her chest, behind her eyes, but it wasn't stomach cancer or the death of a child. This was what, love? She broke up with a girlfriend? What a laugh. She was lucky.

Certainly she was lucky tonight. Look at that. She won another round, pulling the chips to her, laughing. Was she up to her old tricks? Dealing from the bottom with the expertise of the ancient tricksters? Nah. That'd been the celebrity surgeon, the con artist, the saleswoman, the most popular Avon lady on the block.

No Willy Loman for *Celebrity Plastics*. The surgeon could *sell*. She could take anyone on anything. Used to, anyway. Whatever happened to her, the old dog? Melanie was taking the next card, throwing the one after that, winning that round, and the next. It was so easy, really nothing to it. But the voice was pulling at her.

There are always more than two choices.

Stay or go. Live or die. These are illusions, not paths.

Who said that, she wondered, as the drink came around again, and other substances with it, to chew or smoke or swallow or snort or shoot or lay on your tongue like a vow unspoken and dissolving. Melanie held them in her hand but passed them on without partaking, because that was not her road this time. She wanted a clear head. She was listening, not to the crowd, but to herself.

But isn't that what she'd come for? To obliterate the mind? Turn it off?

I had to get rid of Dylan, Melanie thought. Pride was part of it, but there was more. I'll never be part of the unenhanced human race. My DNA has been altered permanently. I'll forever be different, will live on a separate plane and have to work to be on theirs, squash myself down, shrink what I see to their playing field. The Regenerator changed everything. I'm trapped. I may never die the way they do, but I have to act as though I will, pretend that the great punishment is death, while I know the opposite is true. The punishment is having to see it all through to the end, and then somehow keep going.

An immortality project, that's what I am.

It came to her at last, just as the dawn broke and the light came wafting in, crawling over the tables, up the canvas walls, people asleep around her on the benches or curled in corners on the sand floor. She, meanwhile, in the midst of all that light, she, sitting there, being human and nothing else, her winnings piled in chips around her, like a cowboy of another era. It was then, amid the plastic gold, the collapsed bodies, that it came to her, that *she* came for her. The woman in shadow, the light shining on Melanie, into her, while the woman contemplated some new piece of Melanie that was imperfect. The celebrity surgeon was an artist. You could pull up, or you could fill out, she'd say. You could hide, or you could punch out. You could enhance the skin, or you could pull elsewhere—tight, tight—a foot away, and watch the reverberation across the body. There are so many choices.

You could accept. You could embrace. That's a choice too. The surgeon had said that. You could enfold the error. Choose it. Prize the broken part. The error might be a gift, she'd said.

How had Melanie forgotten?

After the taping was over, the recovery room was always the best of times. Lying on the most comfortable recliner in the world. The props assistant beside her, kind and funny and calm. Old episodes of the show projected so huge and high on the wall, they seemed to come in from the sky, from outer space.

The props assistant had kissed her one night. They'd spent the night in her trailer and Melanie had promised to come back for her, but she hadn't.

Dylan. Regret swept through her. She was not feeling the rush of the run, but sadness. Dylan, a little like the props assistant, actually. Dylan, who knew Melanie was human and treated her as such all along. Dylan, not so easily replaceable. Melanie had thrown her away, why? Why was Melanie's plan to wander solo this lonely Earth? Why would she want to? Why did she think she had to?

A window in her mind opened to the future, and closed. This happened to her sometimes. A side effect of the Regenerator, the future flashing and fading. As she put down a card, she glimpsed it. A window sprang wide, then shut. And another and another. Colorful, murky, streaking, and gone. Some she recognized—she'd seen these flashes before. Others were unfamiliar. Landscapes so strange they seemed impossible, of other worlds, perhaps. Some were just darkness or water. Some were clear.

There she is, in a desert, surrounded by garbage.

There, she's talking to a robot who is singing a song.

There, a small blue compass, glinting on a cloth in the sand.

Later, years later, when Melanie is old, older, she will say of this night that even in that moment, she knew what she would do next. She could see it in the cards, she could see it in the stars, in her tea, on her palms—in all the places you've been warned you might glimpse truth, answers, fate, the future. She knew her nonmechanical steps would take her out of that place, not the next day or the next. A few weeks, a month, two months would pass while she sat and thought and paced and picked up the cards, both the ones she'd been dealt and those she had chosen, before she'd screw up her courage and leave the oasis. She'd go in the night, ride a piece of old construction equipment, bought with her earnings. A cement mixer, a seat open to the air, a monstrous relic churning behind it. Large, yellow, snailish, tires up to her waist. She'd screw up her courage, snail-ride the road west over deserts linked by thin trails through the sand, crawl away from one contaminated coast and toward another, make a beeline (though there were no free bees anymore) through the scrub, the rising sun alighting on her arms, her face, her hands, her chest, on all the skin she'd protected for so long. Days would go by. There'd be hills, abandoned towns, careening hopes, while a clear beam shone down and through her. She'd see the whole organism, all its parts moving together, sliding like blood through veins, and her part in it, her own belonging on this mutt planet. She thought she didn't belong, but she did.

She'd glide toward a molecular collections lab.

All this to come.

She never asked to live forever. Whatever came next was her plight. Perhaps her face would hold it all. Her body, too, would pack it all in. A miracle. Maybe the wrinkles would come but not the explosion. Maybe the Regenerator would do its job—that CRISPR tech is no joke, powerful as kryptonite, sucking the strength out of decay. She could see it. Consider the genius of the surgeon, who put in those first stabilizing implants, solid as limestone, a bedrock. Maybe fiberglass, plastic, and sand aren't so different from fat, meat, bone, and cartilage—the original filler—and can be swapped out if you do it slowly enough, cell by cell. The miracle of life on an exchange.

Meanwhile, on that first night at the oasis, with gold made of not-gold piled around her and her courage a speck of sand (which grain by grain is stronger than you think, can withstand anything this Earth can subject it to—water, wind, pressure, fire—it may melt, it may chip, it may fall out of sight, but it will go on), she pulled the not-gold to her and won it all.

It's all you, robot lady. It's beautiful, startling you. Light-filled, lowered by angels, you, getting ready to arrive.

11

But Dylan didn't know any of that. She returned to the lab.

"Had yourself a good time, then?" said Dr. Das.

She was glummer than ever, slumped in her chair.

Dr. Das sighed. "So you heard the news, I take it." He spread his hands. "I'm sorry."

"News?" She lifted her head an inch.

Dr. Das lowered his hands. "Do you never check your messages?"

Dylan slid farther into her seat.

"Go check your goddamn messages."

She crept out.

She scrolled, saw nothing of interest, until she spotted a company video memo from Sea Garden, a customer representative, a real person, not an AI. She opened it, watched the message. A young man tugged at his collar and said that since her mother was gone—or, rather, her body was still there but not her per se—he was calling to discuss arrangements, not for her *effects*, those had been—

She clicked on the link and after a while of pressing *person*, *person*, *person*, a different face appeared, an empty name tag floating over it.

"What do you mean, 'gone'?" she said. "What do you mean 'effects'?"

The reception was bad. The top half of his head was slightly out of alignment with the lower. "One moment while I pull up your account," he said. "It says here—according to Dr. Stein's final instructions . . ."

Dylan found she couldn't breathe. "I don't understand." A flash of her mother alone in the pod. "She was perfectly healthy. Was there an accident?" She fought to stay calm. "How did she die?"

The admin sighed. "Well, she didn't die now, did she." The video zzzed for a moment. His head sliced clean in two, then he was back. "—your transport?"

"Sorry, what was that?"

The admin cleared his throat. "Shall the company arrange your transportation?"

Dylan closed her eyes, placed a finger between them. "The bit before that. If she didn't die, where is she?"

"Dr. Stein was transferred."

"Ah." She breathed out. "Where to?"

The admin blinked a few times. "A microchip." Dylan's face must have shown her confusion, because he added, "She was relocated to a solar kite. Outer space. You didn't know?"

She scanned her mind. "No."

"I'm sure she'll be in touch," he assured her.

"In . . . touch?" She considered this for a while. "So she's coming back?"

"Oh, no, certainly not. Her body—" The admin shook his head. "It's not possible."

Her body. A drop of sweat slid down her back.

"I believe you're supposed to receive letters." He seemed uncertain.

"How . . ." She trailed off. She looked away from the screen at the vials of sand and plastic models on her desk.

"Will you be making your own arrangements, then?"

She looked back to the screen. "For her body?"

His eyes glazed, reading something she couldn't see. "We have here that you will be taking her place."

"In her *body*?"

The admin let out a little yelp. "The pod. It belongs to you."

She blinked. "At Sea Garden?" An image of it rose before her—beige-green walls, windows of dark dead sea, monthly deliveries from above. She shook her head. "I don't want it."

"It's a luxury model."

"You can keep it."

The admin sucked in his breath. "Please hold." His face switched off and she stared at his hold-screen, a basin of fake fish floating. A flood of blood and water and sand began to fill her mind. She tried to recall her mother's last message. Had she read it? When was the last time she read one of her mother's messages? Had she written back? The admin's face reappeared. "Are you saying you want to sell it?"

Her mind was still lagging a few steps behind, dragging. "Her *body*?"

Again, the shocked cry. "The *pod*." He enunciated the word with care.

"Oh, sorry." She lowered her forehead to her fist. "Yes, I want to sell it."

She sat in her room beside the vials of sand, her hands clenching and unclenching on her desk. Days went by. She entered a period of hesitant mourning. Her mother's status was still unclear to her, so her grief was stuttering, incomplete, arriving in fragments. Was it *her* alive on the chip? Or was she dead, and some robotic, demonic copy of her brain was out roaming the universe? How did they extract her? And what had happened to her *body*? Was it frozen in a vat or destroyed? Had they killed her? How? It was disgusting and mortifying.

She was truly alone in the world now.

She managed to set up an appointment with the "lead researcher" on the "experimental research team" (the arrogance and the sheer inanity of those terms). The man who might have killed her mother appeared on the screen with so many filters turned on, she wasn't sure if he was a human or a cartoon.

"Which piece of her exactly was—what is the word—'uploaded'?"

"Ah, yes! Good question. No. An upload is different." A grotesque grin. "An upload is a backup. You enter a local space. You join others."

"So my mother is with these other . . . people?"

"No, same software, but she was *transferred*. She is on a solar kite. That's an independent chip."

"So she is not . . . backed up."

"No."

"And why is that?"

He shrugged. "Some people don't want to. It can cause confusion. One there, one here. Which is the real one?" He let out a bark. No, that was a laugh.

"I see," she said numbly. His head looked like a balloon she could pop with two fingers. "And you sent the only . . . copy . . . of my mother into outer space."

"We don't call it a copy, but yes, in a way, the general idea is correct."

"May I ask the purpose of this . . . transfer?"

"Experimental research."

"Yes, I got that bit. Could you be more specific?"

"It's space exploration. Others may follow. It may be a solution."

"A solution to what? We found solutions already. We solved!

Everything got worse." She could crush his face into gel. "Why are you people always looking for solutions? We don't need any more solutions."

"Whoa." He held up his hands, which looked bizarrely long, modified. "This was Dr. Stein's idea. Her life's work."

Her eye twitched. "No."

"The transfer of human consciousness. She worked on that code for decades. Her greatest achievement. Perhaps humanity's greatest achievement."

She shook her head.

He leaned toward the screen. "She chose this."

"Did she choose not to keep a copy?"

He grinned. "Maybe she thought no one wanted one."

That hurt.

When she got off the call she realized he hadn't answered any of her questions.

She was unable to leave her room. It felt like the early days, the noise in the hallway, the footsteps, too loud. She didn't go to work. The researchers knocked on her door, asked if she was all right. Word had gotten out. They all knew. When she didn't respond, they stood in the hallway murmuring words of sympathy or encouragement through the door, while she lay on her cot with a pillow over her face. Through the roar in her mind, she saw her mother, drifting, passing by Mars and other planets, getting farther, smaller. At last the researchers went away, left her alone, alive.

So her mother's trip to see her *had* been a goodbye. But Dylan hadn't said goodbye to her, not really. That got to her. Why hadn't her mother told her, been direct about it, instead of creepily turning up at the center, abruptly departing, leaving a long tail of cryptic messages, epistles, really, who could get through them? Dylan hadn't responded—she realized, scrolling—to her last three messages. And the one before that, she'd answered with a smiling dolphin waving. Good god, she was a barbarian. But who wrote letters like these anymore? You had to spoon through them like a chunky word soup to find what you wanted. Her mother had always been so silent when Dylan was growing up, who knew she'd had so much to say?

Dylan lay on her cot, shade pulled down over the window. Her mind sifted through its accumulated debris, the discarded past, the file folders and trash bins of her consciousness. As a child of depop, her mother had lost *everyone* (but so had everybody else). She'd brought Dylan to Sea Garden to keep her safe (was that true?), and Dylan had left with the agreement that she would come back, at least to discuss it, but she had not and never intended to, had lied to her mother's face (this, though the old arguments against her mother were pushing upward, rising to the surface). And when her mother came to visit, Dylan had been cold, critical, withholding, had not insisted that her mother stay with her at the center. Worse, Dylan had not listened. She might have told her if Dylan had given her a chance, pushed a little more. She might have stayed.

No, Dylan knew better. Her mother had planned this all along. A terrible revelation.

But—and this did give her an iota of solace—she saw, scrolling through her messages, popping them open, grazing, that she'd only pretended to lose touch. Her mother had continued the conversation regardless, like a radio playing to a sleeping person, some of it getting through, because here were familiar bits, such as this, a description of the monthly delivery gone wrong. Dylan remembered reading that and laughing. (The woman had a sense of humor when she felt like it, Dylan could give her that.) Or here Dylan had written three full sentences in response. Or here Dylan had sent six screenshots of her DNA models, along with a question, and she'd read her mother's thoughtful response, her articulation of Dylan's ideas about the possibilities of sand as a way to preserve molecular life. So Dylan *had* read her messages, some of them, or at least scanned them, and the familiar ones gave her some comfort (though would it have killed her to answer a few more of them?). She read the messages over and over. She recalled now the fleeting thought that her mother *would* eventually give up and come live at the lab, which Dylan had been dreading, if she was honest, but who doesn't dread their mother coming to live with them? And why hadn't she done that, like a normal person, instead of catapulting some theoretical version of herself into outer space on a silicon microscrap?

During the peak day hours, while the rest of the place slept, Dylan scrolled and scrolled, down, down, down, through her messages and saw—because it was right there—that her mother had told her, had laid it out amid swaths of scientific patter, had explained the whole plan and why, all her intolerable reasons, her shortsighted, misplaced, exhausting trust in human invention. How sad, depressing, absurd. She could barely read it.

Her mother believed in life, the abstract concept, not lives, the individual entities—such her own self, which she let be shot off like space trash. Or her own daughter, who had always been an experiment, a failed one at that, part of her endless, infuriating project to expand all life. Her retort to depop. Her emotional data was static. Her mother wasn't moving forward. She was going backward, fighting Earth with acrylic and nanometals, hurrying the death of Earth, not the healing of it.

Before she closed the file, Dylan did see with relief that her mother did not blame her. She had never been that sort of person, Dylan knew, petty or spiteful, and this hurt even more.

Dr. Das summoned her. She wasn't sure how much time had passed. A week. Two weeks. She left her room, softly padded down the hallways and around a series of right angles, went through air lock after air lock, donned her biosecurity suit, soaked her shoes in disinfectant, wrapped her hair, waved away the man at security. Flickers of Melanie accompanied her. She walked along the line of repulsive cryochambers. She'd never liked the cryochambers, and now they seemed implicated, if not directly to blame.

She followed Dr. Das into his office, slouched in a chair.

He sighed. "I know it's rough."

She forced a nod.

He tapped a fidget and watched some lights move around on the pad. She bet he felt a little sorry for himself, being left with her on his hands.

He cleared his throat. "What about your father? You don't have any contact with him, do you?"

She straightened a little, before sinking back down. Who was her father? She'd never known. Had there even been one?

"Well, these things take time."

Another nod.

"Your mother is a pioneer. You can be proud."

She pushed down the urge to get up and shove him off his smug specialty desk chair. She said as casually as she could, "Did you know?"

"No." He tapped the fidget and the lights went off. "I suspected she had a project, but I didn't know what."

She wasn't sure if she believed him.

"I want you back on duty."

"I quit."

"It's not good to hide in your room, you know."

"I resign. I'm officially giving notice. I don't want to work here anymore."

"Landscape duty. It'll be good for you."

In fact she had nowhere else to go. She went back to work, left her room in the dark. The sand had built up in her absence. Mounds of it stretched along the walls like long shadows. She shoveled it, cleared it away, carted it through the night.

She went outside the walls with a wheelbarrow and brought back in rocks. She arranged them in paths, left a smooth white puddle of sand around the facility like a silvery island. Sand that had constructed and deconstructed every world this Earth has known, made up of elements that had come from as far as her mother was heading.

Traces.

The life it contained and did not.

Dylan's own permeability, her own none-ness.

She herself made up of these same traces. She, a container of outer space that had been stuck on this planet for so, so long, combining and recombining into life and not life. But that, too, was an illusion: Earth was *in* outer space, churning through the galaxy. Humans always made that same tedious mistake, believed themselves to be the great exception, forgetting that when they observe the sky they observe themselves. All that is stuck here will come unstuck, she thought. If we just wait, if we're not in such a goddamn hurry, we don't need to go to great lengths to get away. We will be sent back out, regardless of our desire or form or condition. There's no rush to spread or destroy ourselves. We will be knocked into pieces, sucked into the sun, exploded back out.

She thought of Melanie (would she ever see her again?). She

picked up the rake and walked back outside the walls. She looked across the desert. Dawn was winking into the present, lighting up the sand in pastels and metallics. Some of it was moving—a mirage? But no. As she stood there, the mirage swelled and turned into a parade. Figures, people, emerged from the luminous sand, grew from it. Their clothes and baggage were the shade of sand, their skin and hair coated with it. They were walking along the horizon. She'd never seen such a sight in this wild desert.

My god, she thought, it's the sand people. She'd heard of them but she'd been told they were long gone. They were on foot, but they seemed to be pushing a thin motorbike with a person on it. They paused and beckoned to Dylan. She couldn't tell if they were real or if she was dreaming them. They called out. One walked a few steps toward her and gestured for her to come. She dropped her rake and went to them.

3

Exit Earth

12

We are twenty-five, but this morning we added a new one. We came upon her in front of a large bleached structure, a final outpost of concrete, steel, and glass.

We've been walking five days already, first through the scrub, then the company dump, a hundred miles of it. Slow through the "recyclables" because we slid around on the plastic bottles and because of all the stuff we're carrying—and, of course, because of the bike. On the fourth night the plastic lessened, gave way to rubble and rocks, and at last we saw sand. We walked toward it.

Then today at dawn we found her. She was outside raking sand (which, really, why?). We called to her. I walked a few strides in her direction. Our leader nodded to me to keep going. My sandals left a single line of soft imprints. I could see her faded shirt, her ballcap. She put down her rake and came to us. Many of us joined in a similar manner.

She hasn't spoken yet, but she drinks from the canteen we left for her on a rock. Each time we stop, she moves in a little closer. We leave her a reflector to rest under. She's still there when we start up again that evening.

We take turns pushing our leader on her bike. She sits on the seat, while two of us hold on to the handlebars and push, digging our heels into the sand. Sometimes a third presses from behind. When my turn comes, I push for hours, sand and sweat coating my face, my hair swinging in a long rope down my back, my brown pants loose and brushing the ground. I stop only to wipe my eyes with my forearm. When we come to a large dune or a deep rut, one of us straddles the bike, starts the engine, and rides a few hundred feet, our leader holding on to their shoulders. "We are not masochists, after all," says our leader. There's petrol in the tank and a few gallons in the supplies.

On our next break, our leader calls to the newcomer. She approaches, hat pulled low, and we gather around. "Word has spread about our project," our leader says. "Here is proof." She gently turns the newcomer toward us. "Now it is only a matter of time." The newcomer stands quietly. I'm not sure how much she understands. She doesn't seem to speak our language, or perhaps any language. She nods, which is at least respectful.

We go on.

Of course, there have been any number of suicide missions throughout history, a handful of citizens who together decide they are done. Because they are turning themselves into bombs. Because they believe they will be shuttled into an asteroid by magic and traveled through outer space. Because their murderous god told them to. Because plague, protest, madness, revenge. Because the new world didn't arrive. Or it did and it was worse than the old one. Because it's all too hard. Us? At least ours is right and good. We believe (correctly) that humans are a blight and should be eradicated from Earth. Voluntarily remove ourselves from the destruction.

You may say that with only twenty-five of us, we're not going to put much of a dent in the thing. There are still millions left on the planet, supposedly, and who knows how many on Mars, if that's still happening. A little late on the draw, if you really want to know, but at least a statement.

Stop repop. Finish the job. Set an example.

Night again, day again. Beige brightening. Overhead, white. "We seek a new baptism," our leader shouts. She raises a fist. "Of sand, not water. Death, not life. We let go of the rot of civilization and head into the purity of empty sand. We return to the unknown.

"Woe to triumph," she says.

"We seek defeat!" we call.

"Woe to expansion."

"We seek contraction!"

"Woe to life."

"We seek death!"

"Inevitable as it is right." Our leader raises her arms. "We do our part to hasten the uncrowding of our species. Remove at least these few. Us, together."

"Us, together!"

The great expanse of garbage stretches behind us. The desert opens ahead. Is this it, is this it? I think. Am I ready, am I ready, am I ready? Light bounces off the rocks. The newcomer moves in a little closer.

But instead of dying, we go on.

We've been walking a week now, pushing our leader through the sand. She is royal, ashy, old. Her hair is in cords like fingers, her voice a rasp. An accident years back left her limping. A year ago, a stroke. Walking is difficult. We bring her. We pass signs of fallen civilization. Things the sand buried and the wind half unburied. Ancient houses that look like they grew out of the sand and then collapsed. A fossilized gas station blasted white. Must have marked the spot of a highway long ago. Farther up, we find evidence of a former town, tops of houses. We make a few wisecracks. Civilization got what it deserved, that kind of thing. But our leader shushes us. "Silence. Grieve this lost community." She moves us through. We bow our heads but she brightens, tells us stories about the people who lived here and flourished during their time. It is in moments like these that I love her most—her charisma, her calm, her vision.

She urges us on.

The dunes turn the world into a simple geometric shape: the curve. There is no right angle, certainly no rectangle. "The rectangle is an idea we imagined and made," our leader tells us. "We have made so many by now that they've become more real to us than anything else. But can I tell you a secret?" She leans in. "They don't exist."

Today an entire ridge slides when we place a foot. We find ourselves up to our thighs and have to wriggle out or be tugged out.

But where is our leader? Is she all right? We see she is above us with the newcomer, who has maneuvered the bike around the dune. Our leader is in good spirits. "No sinking!" she calls out with her illuminated smile. "No dying today!" she jokes.

We titter wearily, though our laughs come out as gasps and end in coughing. The drifting sand has gotten into our lungs and we are pulling down our masks and spitting up globs of yellow mucus and blood.

The newcomer shows us with gestures where to go—it seems she is mute. Who knows how long she has been out in this desert.

We reach the top of the dune. Below is a sky-filled basin, dust. Our eyes are drying out. Our liquid bodies feel fragile. How much farther? We shield our faces against the blowing sand.

Then there's the sun, that bitch. The sun hates us, that much is clear. We are squinting and suffocating. But what are you going to do? It's the end-time. Every part of the planet is done with us: the air, the ground, the water. They've had it with humans.

"But never underestimate humans," our leader says. "You have to stamp out every ember."

The newcomer is wily, wanders ahead, or off in a different direction over the dunes, then jogs back easily to catch up. I'm worried about whether she can commit. This is the sort of project where you have to be all in or all out. I go over to our leader. "The newcomer keeps going off by herself. I'm afraid she'll get lost."

"What do you suggest, Teresa?" she says. That's me, the name she gave me.

I consider. "Perhaps we should tie her hands and lead her." I don't know what makes me say that. She studies me for a while and I squirm.

I think of Moe. He was my recruit long ago. He managed to fade out of the picture so slowly it was like he evaporated. He missed a meeting, then another meeting, his awkward empty mat beside mine. I tried to confront him, cornered him outside his complex. He examined the pavement with immense interest, drew a circle with his toe, and finally admitted, "I'm not going to make it tonight. I'm going to stay in and play Bolly Ball on my Cue." Oh, lowly, wormy, lumpy Moe!

I wanted to bring him back in a muzzle but our leader said we couldn't force him.

A message passes back to those of us who have fallen behind. We'll stop here. Continue on tomorrow. We drop our packs where we stand, lie on the ground. We pull our scarves over our heads. We are humans, after all, not the nomadic desert pigs of yore.

We're still alive hours later when the motorcade overtakes us. We spot it from a distance, a dark squiggle and a rolling cloud of dust. They're headed toward us. Our leader signals us to rise. She stays quiet, a fist pointed toward the squiggle. "Line up," she says softly. "They've come." And we understand they've come to stop us, to plead with us to return, help preserve the human race.

We quickly assemble. I reach for the newcomer, stand her beside me, her scarf wrapped expertly around her face. "We must be bold," our leader says, standing a bit wobbly in front of her bike. "I will speak first, then you will each have time to make a statement." We are bleary but determined. The motorcade zooms up, stops. There are about a dozen of them. Their giant capes ripple in the wind. They have on the white company helmets of a scientific inquiry team, the sort our leader scoffs at. ("That's all we need—*more* science!") They have on oxygen tanks, which we covet. We want to please our leader, but we can't help but see ourselves as we must appear to these strangers: our dirty faces, our broken shoes. They rotate their helmeted heads back and forth down our line, like iridescent insects gathering data.

Our leader takes a step forward, lifts an arm, and starts to speak. I can't hear her clearly over the wind and idling engines. I can make out only vowel sounds, round as stones. She says hardly a few words before the one at the front points down the line. We freeze. Which of us do they want? Who did they come for? Some of us would be missed, others of us are wanted. It seems as if the gloved finger is pointing in my direction. Could it be the newcomer? Who is she anyway? I can't let them take her. My mind spins (could it be *me* they want?). Fear and hope intertwine. Our leader has fallen silent. They rev their engines. They drive down our line in the direction of the finger, blowing sand over us. They ride around us as if around boulders and keep going.

So that's it, then. They didn't come to carry us back, kicking and screaming, to the compound. As they disappear over the dunes, we see they are transporting a cache of boxes, who knows where or why. They are after something else in that sand. No one cares we're here at all. Maybe no one knows. Our leader starts saying this, speaking for us. "Maybe no one knows we're here at all!" she cries with a despair so real, for a moment we believe her and feel a wall of anguish fall down on us. Then she chuckles, and we smile with relief. "Ah, well. You could say the same for the rest of the Great! Human! Experiment!" she says, throwing out her arms. She leans back and shouts into the sky, "Alone in the universe! Poor me!" We laugh and laugh, fall onto the sand. We sit up, sigh, and watch the caravan fade away, the cloud of dust following. The newcomer, I see, is facing the other way. So is our leader.

The next morning I wake in the desert and open my eyes with this thought: If we all had sandbikes, some of us would have turned around and gone home by now. Mutinied or deserted. As it is, no one could change their minds and hope to make it back alive.

Except the one who steals our leader's bike.

The thought tumbles through, pushed by wind.

We are walking into the hottest part of the day when it begins. Our leader stops and signals to us to kneel. We've arrived. At what? It's a space like any space. Silent, soft dunes in every direction. One by one we copy our leader, lower to the ground, and put our faces in the sand. I pull the newcomer down, perhaps a bit roughly. A long line of us in a circle around our leader. A pile of rags in the dust. Today, animated. Tomorrow, not.

We set up the blanket as it gets dark, unroll it over the sand. It's the size of a tapestry. We sewed it with our own hands. It took months, and just to see it brings back the blue tiles and cool rooms of the compound, our leader telling stories, like she did when she and I were kids and I was her only follower. She was already wise then and talking about death.

In one corner of the blanket, the galaxy begins. It bursts out in a wide spin across the fabric, a glittery spray of space dust, meteorites, stars, and merges in the middle with the great universe of bacteria and amoebas. At the other end is our small solar system, the plants, animals, and a few simple symbols marked along the edges to indicate us, humankind. We take off our sandals and step onto the cloth. It feels smooth and cool on our burned, calloused feet. We run our hands over the tiny stitches that we took such pains with. Our leader sinks onto the blanket beside me, presses her cheek into the pale silk moon. We all lie down. We are like silver fish scattered at odd angles on a beach. We stare up at the galaxy from our galaxy of cloth and beads and from inside our own restless, mutable inner galaxies. The newcomer comes over and sits on a corner of the blanket, her feet in the sand.

I fall asleep for a while. I guess we all do, we're exhausted. I dream of a pale beam of light sliding through our camp. I wake, lift my head, half dreaming that I see the little sand bike roaring away, but it's silent. The air is wavy with heat. Then I really do see a flicker on the horizon. A figure out there, a person.

We are ambushed, I think, by pirates!

Or, no, it's the company! They've come to convince us!

We are saved! (Why would I think *that*?)

Or—and my airdreams deflate—it's one of us out there.

It is. It's the newcomer, exploring like a child, her last day on Earth, crouching over the ground, drawing with a stick. She seems so free.

I go out and lead her back. She comes along quietly.

Sand, on the move, always shifting, changing, never the same, like that river, like oneself. Sand, the origins, arrived here in meteorites containing all the ingredients needed to make us. Still living, full of gifts, nutrients.

The newcomer is still there when we get up. We set out the last meal, opening the remaining tins. "Don't save it!" our leader says. It is something she's always said to us. "Save nothing. Use it all up or give it away." But it was never about food. It was about love or material goods or life itself. Now we see she was imagining this meal all along. She imagined saying those words here, and us understanding. We swoon with happiness. We eat, feeding each other and getting juice on our hands and faces.

Then she hands out the capsules. We know a song about the future and we sing it, swaying: trees filling cities, insects flying, the air clearing, concrete sinking like a swamp. My head is buzzing. She beckons me to come receive my capsules and blessing. I go to her with trembling hands. With the last of the water, everyone drinks the capsules down as the moon rises.

But the bike: That's what I'm thinking about. It's easy to figure out who will steal it. Where do you get the betrayer? Look to the loyal. That's where the muddy psychologies lie, in the people unflinching in the face of crazy ideas. There's got to be a complicated tower behind those locked eyes, a tower built of objects easily toppled—tin cans, loose blocks, cardboard—held together by spit, Scotch tape, glue sticks, defiance. It's the loyal one who has so much to lose, who has given up too much, has motivations that are unknowable, perhaps even to herself. She is the one to keep your eye on. Who knows when she might lose the ability to plug up the holes, when the waters of rage or confusion will flood in and knock everything over. Who knows what might trigger it, cause a sudden shift in allegiance. Then what will she do? Will she resign herself, take the path of least resistance? Die with the sheep?

Or will she thumb the capsules into the sand, push them in, and rise like the lions of lore, or like that bitch the sun?

She will.

I do. Because the loyal one has no ideology. From the first day I crawled out from under the slide in the playground, six years old, and went over to the leader, I was always only trying to save my own life.

I am wily. We dance, sing, pray. I weave through with the nonchalance of the loyal, nod in my best imitation of our leader. I turn. I will have a single minute, maybe two.

But just as I begin to step off the blanket, make my escape, I hear the roar of the bike's engine. Wait, who could it be? I scan the group on the blanket. Some of them are already vomiting into the sand. Who is missing? Then it hits me: I was so distracted, she slipped away! And I see, we all see—because she rides right through us—the newcomer. Waving at us and grinning like a lunatic.

I lift my arms in horror and rage—and I see a capsule still stuck to my hand.

"She has betrayed," I scream, though the capsule on my hand shows that I have too.

"No," our leader says, "hush. She didn't. I gave it to her."

"You *gave* it?" I scream.

"It's all right," our leader says. "We don't need that old bike anymore!" How she laughs as she says it! "She wanted to go home," she says. Then she sees the capsule, because I still have my hands spread in despair and madness. "Oh," she says. "I'm sorry. I didn't know. Why didn't you tell me? You could have gone with her." Our leader (Heidi is her name, Heidi Krantz) reaches for me. "I thought you were home."

I pull away. I sink into the sand.

Life. It is not an experiment. There is no one on the other side, working the levers, dropping the pellets, recording the results. Even if there were, we could never know, could never thank them, not really, for this gift. Could never look into their face and tell them what it meant to us to be here. We are forever hidden from each other. I get up and stumble after the bike, choking on sand. I fall to my knees, scarf blowing over my head. I gasp for air.

Around me I hear the chorus. It is my friends, my partners on this path. They are calling out their names, the ones our leader gave them, introducing themselves to the next world, using their voices. "My name is Tom." "I'm Francine." "I'm called Tree." "Hello, I'm Patricia, they call me Patty. Are you there?"

I lie in the sand, feel the next world approaching, but I'm still stuck on this last one. My name is not Teresa. It's Dell, for Delilah, and I'm not welcoming the next world, I'm clinging to the last. Thank you for this blip, this dot, this tiny moment, thank you for letting me lie here, breathing in sand, soaking in the radiation of our own making. Even this, I'll take it. I'll take it, I'll take it, I'll take it.

13

"But you lived," said the Martian. He lifted his drink to look at the brown, misty swirl. Years had gone by.

"Yes, well, they came for us."

"Who? The next world?" He took a sip, frowned.

"The company. The drones picked up our location and dispatched a rescue team."

"But the poison?" said the Martian.

"I didn't take it. Everyone died but me. By the time they arrived, I was surrounded by corpses."

He nodded. "You sure this was her?" He held up his device.

"It was a long time ago, but, yeah, that's her."

He tapped his device and slid it over. "Was this the path you took through the dump?" He drew a line with his finger.

She examined the map for a while. "How should I know?"

The Martian looked up at the wall. Three analog clocks were all stopped on different times. "What happened to her?"

"Our leader? She died. It was awful."

"The newcomer."

"Oh, I never saw her again."

The Martian, Zee, signaled to the bartender. He paid his tab and hers, stood up from the bar, stepped out into the desert. He walked straight across the sand for twenty Earth minutes and arrived at a silver tube rising out of the ground. He got in, pressed a sequence of twenty-six numbers from memory, and wrapped the straps to his body. For the next hour he stood, thinking. Then he popped open the door to the tube and greeted his colleagues. He was shaking. “She’s alive,” he said.

14

The Final Song of Heidi Krantz

As Heidi died, she recalled a river. She remembered the sensation of submersion, the weightlessness and coolness. She was sinking into the river now, she felt, though she knew it was sand. But it felt like water lit with bubbles and froth, and she was going down, down.

But, wait, she was forgetting something.

Delilah, she thought. Delilah will be all alone.

When the company security forces came and rounded them up all those years ago, the men said there would be ice cream where they were going. There would be toys and school. And when the kids scattered out of their sight and reach, the security forces called to them, said that their parents were waiting for them, and the kids halted in their tracks. "Your parents have ice cream and they're waiting for you. Come get on the bus," they called, waving. But Heidi knew that her parents were dead.

She could see that the security forces were going to take them one way or another. It could go this way, the fun way, or the other way. She didn't care what happened to herself anymore, but she needed to think about the others, so she came out of the drain and walked across the dirt. Because she was the oldest, the others came out too. They all boarded the bus together. She led them in a song as they rode. One about trees growing through the roots of cities. She led them in bus-window games and clapping games. But she couldn't help thinking of the littlest kid, who wasn't among them. The one who was so young and small. She lived under the slide in the old playground. Dirty Delilah, they called her. She had stayed hidden, had not gotten on the bus. Now she was all alone back there, left behind.

On the bus Heidi kept thinking about her.

But Delilah!

A day in and the bus stopped for a break. The kids climbed down and sprayed out over the tarmac. Heidi crawled under the bus and then ran for the river on the other side. She jumped in, heard shouts, shots—she'd been spotted. She sank, swam underwater until her lungs were going to burst. She made it to the other side, crawled through the concrete cones and tubes, hid until nightfall. She began walking back.

Decades later, in the sand, Heidi twitched.

But Delilah!

No, she recalled. That's all over now. That was long ago.

Wrong. It's yet to come. She didn't take the pills!

Why would she stay behind?

She didn't care that Delilah didn't take the pills. She cared that they weren't together.

How should one live, in the end? Leaning over the ledge into the unknown? Or standing at the edge and reaching back toward home?

Her brain was pulling apart, soaking—no, it was drying. The tissue was separating into globs and layers.

But Delilah!

Who's Delilah?

Her memory was spreading, wrecking.

The thought-words were losing their meaning, slowing down, becoming animal sounds, sand sounds, air sounds.

Oooos d ly la

Btttt d lie ya

Oooos d ai yah

U eh ai ya

Until Heidi blinked out and was gone.

15

It was a misunderstanding, is all.

When Dylan saw the parade in the desert, she took them for the sand people. She'd heard stories of the caravans of nomads staying ahead of the company, moving between secret oases in the desert, bringing their homes, their families, or becoming families along the way. She was still crushed by the loss of her mother, crushed by the rejection by Melanie. She'd never really found a place in this world. She was uncertain of so much—but not everything. She glimpsed the sand people and was filled with longing. They beckoned, even the matriarch beckoned. Dylan dropped her rake, fixed her hat and sunglasses, and walked toward them. Whatever their destination, she no longer cared. She trusted that they knew the desert far better than she and knew how to keep her safe. She was right: They took care of her. She tagged along at a distance. The matriarch directed them to provide her with the essentials—water, food, and an ingenious flexible case that opened into a shell to block the sun during rest. Why the matriarch had summoned her, she did not know, and she did not ask or try to find out. For the first couple of days she was plagued by thoughts of her mother, but the heat and the trek soon burned out all thought and she walked in a trance behind the strangers. She followed them deeper into the desert than she had ever been and she observed the behavior of the sand as she never had before, as the tour passed the last scrub and entered the moving, living, working sand dunes. They paraded through ridge after ridge of gentle seifs, their long linear forms and sharp crests advancing like rippling water. They wandered along a colony of barchans, horn-shaped dunes migrating southward, marching, hundreds of them. They saw star dunes branching across the plain in crisscrosses, sending thousands of tons of sand streaming out in swirls. Sand sweeping the hemisphere, following the curve of the planet, mimicking the sky in its vastness and variety, in its ignorance of us. Sand arriving here from across the world, particles and microparticles from other planets, untouched by human hands, made up of the rock that formed before the beginning of life.

Of the sand people (because Dylan still thought they were sand people), only the matriarch spoke much. Sometimes Dylan listened to her teachings, sometimes not. She spoke an unfamiliar dialect Dylan didn't understand, but that didn't bother her, and she barely wondered where they were headed—an oasis out in the sand, she supposed, or perhaps they were going all the way to the other side of the desert, to the old country, a place of trees and wildflowers and rain. Perhaps it still existed. She didn't care where they were going. Her mind was empty and she let it be ground down to a pinpoint, a mote of floating animal energy. But on the third day, she found herself gazing into the sand from behind her sunglasses, and her mind began to move forward without her permission and empty of her own effort or input. The desert began to reveal the sand in ways she had not imagined. The sand was alive, had agency, was already constructing the next Earth. It contained secrets, creatures, kingdoms, and she could hear them. She could hear the sand whistling and booming, drumming, squeaking. The dune tunes. She'd heard of them but had never witnessed their song. Her mind was slowly waking. She observed her mind, as if from a distance, directed her attention loosely where it pointed, but did not engage it, let it pass on by. On the third day she found she began to have an urge to follow her thoughts, as if they were footsteps in front of her, moving softly through the hills, climbing. She approached some of the family members, tried to ask for a few simple tools—a device to type on or even just pencil and paper. They did not reply, likely could not understand her and her pantomimes. So she went on solo hikes to explore and think, while the group rested or sat in their family circle. She tried to make sketches of her ideas and calculations in the sand with her finger, but the grains were too dry to hold her shapes. She filed her thoughts away in her brain but she could feel them eroding in there, blowing away. She didn't mind. In fact she resented their presence. She resented thought returning, because what did thought matter? But the thoughts kept coming back, like an instinct or an itch. Again and again, she found herself lost in thought, her brain working, connecting, building. How to construct it, how to preserve it without nitrogen, ethanol, power? A sandbox, she could imagine it, one that depended only on Earth itself, made up solely of the organic materials around her. She could see it, Earth 7.

One night the matriarch waved her over and signaled the others to leave. She spoke in Dylan's own language, which Dylan didn't realize she knew. The matriarch asked her what she was thinking about when she looked into the sand and when she made her drawings in it. Dylan said she couldn't explain, that she'd like to but it was impossible, for she didn't have the words herself. The matriarch said she and her companions would soon be headed out on a longer journey, going much farther, into an unknown land, free of sand, free of death, a new kind of life, a rebirth, and did she want to come? The matriarch said she hoped she would come, but it was her choice. Dylan thought for a moment—to be free of death, what could it mean? She thought it must be the place beyond the desert, where the rain was said to fall all spring. She was tempted. After all, who was she to save the world or a copy of it to toss into a drawer for a next generation to look askance at? Her mother's legacy, who needs it? As she opened her mouth to respond, she wasn't sure what she was going to say. Then she spoke.

"With respect, I want to go home," she said. "I have to. I don't want to be an inconvenience, but perhaps I could join a caravan heading the other way?"

"There is no other caravan. We are the only one."

"And the one we encountered a day back? The friends with the motorcycles?"

"There are no more friends."

"Oh."

The matriarch was still for a while. Dylan waited. "Take my bike," the matriarch said at last.

Dylan shook her head. "I couldn't. How would you ride?"

"I will no longer need to ride."

"Oh, are you being cured?" It was the only thing Dylan could think to say.

The matriarch smiled. "Yes, I am being cured."

"I am too," Dylan said, and realized it was true.

"I'm glad. I'm sad only that I will not see you fully healed. But I wouldn't keep you with us if you want to go home." She put her hands over Dylan's and clasped them. She took her hands away and left a key. "There is petrol in the second supply cart. Not much. Enough to get you back."

Dylan was surprised she had contraband. "But I have nothing to pay you with."

The matriarch waved that away. "I knew that someone would want to go back and I would not deny them. I did not know it would be you, but I am glad I have the bike for you to have. Take it. I will be more comfortable without it."

Dylan was worried. “If you return next year to the place where you found me, I will be there. I can pay you then.”

She patted Dylan’s arm. “Maybe not in this life, but another.”

“But what if I have no other life?”

She laughed. “Sleep now. Tomorrow night, when we gather in our circle, leave. Tell no one today.”

Dylan knew she meant her family would not approve of her giving away this valuable item, and she bowed her head in shame that she had followed them and could not get herself home.

“Will you know the way?”

“Yes,” said Dylan. She took an item out of her pocket and held it up. A small blue compass.

She returned to her sleepbag feeling a tremendous weight of guilt. Now the matriarch would have to ride in a cart or be carried. But Dylan had to go back. She’d seen the curve of the dune. Her life was just getting started. She understood that now. Her mother’s mistake had been to fight the flow of Earth, not move with it. But there might be another way, a new kind of collection. Leave the cage behind in melted pieces. March onward with the march of Earth. So she followed the instructions. The next night, as she rode away, some ran after her, waving goodbye. One in particular who had shown her the most attention. She called back to them, “I’m sorry, family. I’ll pay you back, Grandmother Matriarch. I’ll pay you all back. If not in this life, then another. May we meet again, family. Thank you, thank you, thank you.”

She did not stop until they were far behind.

She rode back toward the lab. She got turned around in the dunes, had to backtrack, got turned around again. Just as she found her way, she ran out of gas. She walked through the last night with the compass as her guide. She collapsed with the molecular collections lab in sight. The researchers must have been looking out for her and captured her on camera, because she woke to them piling her onto a cloth stretcher and carrying her inside the walls, into the cool center. She was burned, cracked, dehydrated, heatstroked, starved, but alive. When she left the infirmary three days later, she padded into the lab. Dr. Das shut an icy, bubbling vat, looked her over, and sighed. “Nearly killed yourself then.”

She nodded in her paper suit.

“Done with that now?”

“Suppose so.”

“Well, your inheritance came through.” He removed his gloves, wiped his hands on a cloth. “That should help.”

It did help.

She received a nice sum for the pod. Sea Garden was apparently becoming a vault, a place to store valuables, or whatever people were counting as valuables these days. The sale, along with other investments her mother left her, came out to more than she’d expected.

So what should she do with the money? What did she want but didn’t have?

Melanie. *(Melanie!)* She could go back to Vacationland and—

Out of the question. Melanie was not for sale.

(Sharp stab.) Got it.

So what else?

She considered. Nothing. Growing up, it had been the one thing: to open a door and walk out on dry land. She had that now.

No, there was more.

Well, if she *had* to say . . .

Say it.

She wanted a place to do her work.

No better place than right here in the lab. Dr. Das would—

Yeah, but.

What?

She'd never liked the dorm, that feeling of being watched, in the hallway, in the cafeteria.

You mean people? You never liked people?

She'd never caught on to the idea of them, yeah, as much as she had hoped. "Community," "teamwork," all that. Yeah, she didn't much like people. Day in and day out, she was ducking her head and mumbling. There were fewer people at the facility than before, but she was still jarred by them. She needed privacy to do her work.

And what work was that?

She was working on it, okay? She would build it, or try to.

So she bought a bungalow in the desert, an old converted storage container. Rough enough on the outside to be entirely passed over by a roving eye. Inside were two comfortable rooms, a small kitchen, and a trapdoor in the ceiling that popped open. You could go up a ladder, crawl out, and look at the stars. Best of all, there was another door in the floor that opened into a large, cool underground room. It was perfect, or would have been. (She imagined Melanie stepping into the container in a flower dress, turning around . . .) She shook her head to clear it.

Dylan had plenty of money left over. She fixed up the sand bike to ride back and forth through the dunes to her job, added a sturdy rack for supplies, and saddlebags for water. She bought a generator and a backup. She took a few microscopes and some other equipment and samples from the lab, ferried them back through the sand.

She climbed into her underground room and sat down to sketch out her thoughts. She set up her equipment and began doing experiments. The sadness didn't leave but it settled into her and she was calm.

It might be strange to think that in her adult life above she was duplicating her childhood life below, living noiselessly in a room just under Earth's surface, but that wasn't what she was doing. Or at least that's not *all* she was doing.

One morning she was out back at the research center, supervising a water receiving, when Dr. Das called her to the office. She paused the program, turned off the funnels, put away her gloves, and walked around to the side entrance. She went in blinking, her eyes adjusting to the dim interior after the outdoor glaze.

"There's someone here to see you," he said.

She wiped away sweat from her face with her shoulder. "Who?"

16

Melanie could not find it. The secret lab wasn't where it was supposed to be. She rubbed her face with a rag (pulling the skin as she did it—ruining decades of work but she was too tired to do better, and it was so, so hot). She climbed down from the cement mixer to check that the engine wasn't overheating (again). It was making a screeching sound, which couldn't be good. She still had to find a spot to set up camp for the night. If only there were some shade out here. She peered out from under her hand. (She'd lost her hat.) Just scrub and flat land. She hadn't seen a person in six days. She was running out of water.

When she found it at last, pulled up to the gate (this had to be it, right? what else could it be?), she didn't know what to expect. A compound behind a wall, blinding pools of sand, no signs of life. But Dylan had to be in there. She turned off the motor—a dangerous move, sometimes it didn't turn back on. The cement mixer rumbled to a stop. She climbed down from the seat. She got out her bag from the cement compartment. She combed her hair with her fingers, wiped her face, assessed with a hand mirror the damage she'd done to herself on the ride. Grime coated her face and neck. Her back was aching, her limbs numb from the vibration of the cement mixer. She approached the panel in the wall beside the gate. She could see the top half of a building over the wall, a structure of concrete. She rang and waited. It all seemed so unlikely. No one answered. She got back onto the seat and turned on the engine. (It started.) She considered her options. She could turn around and head back. She could keep going the way she'd come, see what was out there. The sky was moving over her. She wrenched the stick into gear, waited. After a while she threw the gear into neutral, turned off the motor, got down. She pressed the panel again. She waited.

Someone buzzed at her through an intercom. She couldn't make out what they said but she called out Dylan's name, not knowing what would happen, and was frankly startled when the gate motored open, revealing a set of connected buildings, glass and walkways and shade. Two very clean, official-looking people emerged. She saw them approach and got back up onto the seat so she would be above them. They spoke to her, kept referring to Dylan as "the groundskeeper," as in "So you've come to see our groundskeeper, have you? Would you mind telling us what this is about?" She sat on the cement mixer and tried to answer their questions. "Wait here," they said and they left her out there for a long time. She almost drove off again. But she was tired and out of water. She just sat there.

They came out again and got her off the cement mixer. They brought her inside. They put her in a small office and closed her in. She waited in there alone. She drank an entire pitcher of water that was sitting on the desk. For the first hour she was glad for the air-conditioning, and little else came into her mind. Every now and then the one called Das opened the door and said a few words to her, such as "Can I get you another glass of water?" or "Could you confirm your company ID number?" and then backed out, shutting the door and locking it. She felt a finger of panic walk gently down her chest but she stayed where she was. They couldn't just leave her there, right? She wasn't a prisoner? Melanie moved to the window, a small square that looked out at the wall. She waited. Another hour went by. Then she spotted her through the window, the solemn girl from Vacationland. She was coming around the side of the building, rubbing dust from her hair, sweeping sand from a white work shirt with her hands, thin and boyish—almost a stranger. What was Melanie doing here? A few minutes later the man opened the door and the girl walked in, became Dylan.

Melanie got to her feet. She was taller than both of them.

"Do you know this individual?" said the man. He crossed his arms.

"Yes," said Dylan.

None of them moved.

"You told her our location?" said the man.

"Yes."

He rocked on his heels. "That's a dismissible offense."

"Her directions were terrible," Melanie agreed.

Nothing on Dylan's face told her what she was thinking. Did she still want Melanie? Was this a catastrophic mistake? "I could leave," Melanie offered. "If this is inconvenient."

"Good idea," Dylan said. She put her sunglasses back on. "Let's get out of here." She took Melanie's hand and they left.

17

They slept.

Dylan brought her back to the storage container in a misty trance, rode her over the dunes on her bike, and got her inside. She felt like one wrong word and she would scare Melanie off, so all she said was "Hush," and gave her water. She held her breath while Melanie drank. Her arms and hands were bruised and blistered. Her face was a bit more lopsided, her skin shades darker. Her hair was cut short and fluffed around her face. She had on a khaki shirt and jeans. Dylan had never seen her in anything but a dress. She looked less robotic and somehow younger. "Come here," Dylan said. The two of them curled onto the bed with their clothes on. Dirt fell off Melanie onto the sheet. Her hair was sweaty and tangled.

"I'm tired," Melanie said.

"Me too," said Dylan, because for the first time since her mother disappeared, she *was* tired. She wrapped her arms around Melanie, pulled her to her.

"It's not much," said Dylan. Melanie was strolling around the narrow container, picking up objects and putting them down. "There's a basement." Dylan pointed to the trapdoor in the floor. Melanie opened a cabinet and looked at a row of cans, bags of beans, a sack of rice. She was tall enough that her hair brushed the ceiling. "I didn't know you were coming or I would have picked up some supplies," Dylan went on. Melanie flicked the light off and on. "It's not like Vacationland, but you can get quite a bit."

"They called you a groundskeeper," Melanie said flatly. She picked up a spatula and studied it. "Not a researcher."

"Yes," said Dylan.

"You lied."

"Yes." Then she added, because it seemed honest, "But I am doing research."

Melanie frowned. "What's that up there?" She pointed to the ceiling's trapdoor with the spatula.

Melanie, here! With a spatula. Dylan was blind with desire.

"Stars."

"What kind of stars?"

"The regular kind. Want to see?"

It wasn't a smile that Melanie gave, but it was enough that Dylan unfolded the ladder and crawled out onto the roof into the falling dusk. Melanie followed, hands on the steps, her head emerging. It was enough that they lay down and looked up.

Later that night, Dylan filled a washtub outside and Melanie sat in it. Dylan poured soapy water over her shoulders and down her back, took a washcloth and gently rubbed the dirt from her arms and legs, ran water through her hair. Suds came down her face and chest.

So what do you think? Will you stay? Dylan didn't say, too afraid of Melanie's answer. Her mother had also come and left. She didn't know if she could stand it again.

Towel wrapped, Melanie stepped out of the washtub into the sand.

They pressed together. Touched first at their foreheads and

toes. Then at their lips and breasts, then at their stomachs and thighs, then at their hands and inner forearms. Dylan's clothes, Melanie's towel, dropping. Bare limb to bare limb. Fingers to flesh, tongue to neck, pussy to pussy. They figured it out. Melanie would hang around for a while, decide later. It was decided not to decide.

18

At first the only sound was the sand, which had a whole language, once you listened for it, grains rubbing and moving together. The sounds of Dylan and Melanie came gradually over the days and weeks, first their own rubbing and moving together, then their voices, just short sentences traded ("Wait, move your arm"; "My arm is fine, move your leg"), since they weren't sure yet how to talk to each other in this new space.

Sleeping naked, intertwined on the roof. Waking, turning over, seeing up, seeing out.

Cooking. That was part of it. Staples, mostly. But then Melanie put together an outdoor grill and made a spicy nopales stew.

A ride on the bike to the dump to collect plastics and other garbage they might use. On another day, a ride to get supplies, traveling through wind. Sometimes they drove the cement mixer, but it took twice as long and kept stalling out halfway up a dune. ("I told you this was a bad idea"; "Hey, I like this piece of shit, be nice to it.") Eventually Melanie traded the mixer for a swift solar bike and a sled that hooked to the back.

Will I stay? Melanie wondered.

A slow loosening of their tongues. Traded secrets. ("I may never die"; "My mother's like that too.") Soon, a flood of words between them. Their origin stories and other stories. Mostly about depop. Everyone had lived through it, one way or another.

They found two lawn chair recliners and brought them back. The chairs were holding up pretty well but the vinyl fabric needed reinforcement. Melanie sat in the sand and worked on them all morning. After that they lay on the recliners every night. Sex, stars, sweat, math, eternity, toilets.

She went along one day to the research center. The team greeted her as if she were from outer space—politely, but keeping their distance. The next time, she stayed back at the container. She wasn't lonely. She enjoyed not being looked at. This was a surprise. There were other surprises. She took a walk, picked up some junk she came across, carried it back. A bucket, a stick of wood, a bottle. She set things up and began to play. She'd played as a young person. Her kit grew. She liked to tinker. They grew a percussion junkyard in the sand. Dylan tripped over hunks of metal. "What the fuck is this?" she said, but quietly.

Her body calloused, slimmed. She stopped holding her head with quite the care she had before. She was running a little more natural. "Reckless," she said. "Normal," Dylan said. She clicked in the places where her joints were reinforced, but they held together.

The Regenerator became more pronounced in her jaw as she turned from gym sexy to workwoman muscular: wiry and strong, her implants rising like islands from the ocean. She was getting both further from and closer to being human, she felt. Still, she was beautiful, she knew. Some faces look good no matter what you do to them.

Dylan lay on top of Melanie and felt the purr of the Regenerator.

"I'll tear it out," said Melanie.

"Better not."

"You could watch all the fluid drain out of me. You could water the plants."

"We don't have any plants."

When Melanie fell asleep, glistening under the satellites, Dylan pulled on her shirt and crept down to the underground room.

"You're always working," Melanie said, raising her head.

Dylan paused, hands on the ladder.

Melanie didn't bleed anymore, but for the first time she might have liked to have a child. The feeling swept through her and she let it. It felt good to yearn. She wondered if it was boredom or something else (humanness?) that drove it. It faded.

She didn't decide to stay, but she kept staying.

The dune tunes grew louder as the sand advanced, rolled in like glaciers toward the storage container, would one day reach as far as the lab. The sounds became constant—squeaking, booming, the pattering of sand falling and filling in out-of-sight places. She liked to play along on her improvised drum kit during the long hours Dylan spent in the underground room. At dawn Dylan came up and lay in the sand beside her and listened.

"That's not a song."

"Who cares what it is?"

"It's noise."

"It's music, I'm musical."

"It's a wavelength. It's a wave."

The dunes unfurled around them like they were in a bowl. To be alone with Melanie was not the same as being alone with her mother.

This was the stage in Dylan's life that she began to construct Earth 7 in earnest.

"Explain it. What am I looking at?" Melanie had come down to see.

Dylan showing her. Melanie affixing her eye. Fauna under a microscope. A creature on the slide that looked like an outline, like clear jelly awash in transparent light. It had eight tiny legs. It had claws. It walked like a cartoon. It shone. It had eyes.

"There are more species of animals and plants in sand than in the original rainforest," said Dylan.

"These ones are dead," said Melanie.

Dylan was showing her the other ones.

"They're in tun. They're dried out. They seem dead, but they're alive. Sugar replaced the fluid in their bodies and is preserving them."

"Where did you get these?"

"I scooped them out of the sand."

"Why?" said Melanie. "Fool." But she kissed her.

Really, Dylan's discoveries were elementary. She was no genius. What she figured out had mostly been figured out before. But that was long ago and those researchers were all dead. The remaining researchers were absorbed in other projects or were no longer living in the physical realm at all. But Dylan had been working on this, arguably, since she was six, and arguably her mother had worked on it before her. And Dylan did have something no other researcher had: the sand species of tardigrade.

Her idea was to take a precious strand of DNA from the lab, enclose it in a molecular cuticle, implant it in a tardigrade, let the organism dry out, move into tun. Theoretically it would preserve both itself and the DNA.

She tried it a few times. It didn't work. She tried it a few more times.

Many more times. Months and months.

She got it to work. Some to work. Then some more.

They were like fossils, but alive.

Theoretically the DNA could stay there for hundreds of years, maybe indefinitely.

Theoretically she was designing and constructing an entire molecular collection that needed nothing but dry sand.

Meanwhile, Dr. Das knew nothing about it, because Dylan didn't tell him. She reported to his office.

"Everything going well?" he said.

Which "everything" was he referring to? Everything *was* going well.

"Going good," she said.

"Good, good," he said. "What are you working on out there? You got some special project?"

She startled. "No."

"Uh-huh." Nodding. "And how's . . . ?" He lifted a hand in question.

"Melanie," she supplied.

"She seems like a nice . . ."

"Yes."

Below the surface of Earth, Dylan assembled Earth 7, sample by sample, from DNA dupes she took from the lab. *Balaenoptera musculus*, *Erinaceus europaeus*, *Hippopotamus amphibius*, *Monodon monoceros, Panthera uncia, Ulmus crassifolia, Zaglossus attenboroughi, Centrochelys sulcata, Lycaon pictus, Solanum tuberosum.*

She put in *Ursus maritimus, Eretmochelys imbricata, Elephas maximus sumatranus.*

She put in *Taraxacum officinale, Quercus macrocarpa, Asterias rubens.*

She put in DNA no one would want to clone—*Agkistrodon piscivorus, Ixodes scapularis* (why, Dylan, why?), *Sus scrofa.*

And she added DNA that no one even knew how to clone—*Turdus migratorius, Tyto alba, Rhizanthella gardneri, Isotria medeoloides.*

She spent months, a year, and another year, and another. It went on and on.

Hippocampus zosterae, Partula tohiveana, Bombus distinguendus.

Equus caballus, of course, *Populus tremuloides, Cornu aspersum.*

Ectopistes migratorius.

Cupressus sempervirens.

Adansonia grandidieri.

Gallus gallus.

"I need to show you where I want to bury it," she told Melanie. "You need to know."

"Uh, I really don't."

"In case something happens to me." She meant in case the research lab was looted or destroyed while she was on the premises, or she was buried in an avalanche, or her bike exploded in the heat. It didn't occur to her that she might get sick.

"Fine, take me," said Melanie.

They had to be careful, drones could be tracking them. Dylan taught her the terrain, where the blind spots were, how to throw off observers, how to tell where the sand was unstable. She took

Melanie to the old train car she had plans for, half buried in sand, a barchan growing over it.

“It’ll be in here,” she said. “The dune will cover it.”

They had to climb in through the roof. Melanie walked the floor, hands on hips. “But why?” she said. Dylan shrugged. They brought shovels. They glided Earth 7 over the dunes on the sand sled. They set it up together.

By the time the research lab blew up, blasted into a scatter of fireworks one night, Melanie had been living in the container for over a decade and still hadn’t said if she’d stay. Sometimes love works best that way. Dylan was with Melanie when it happened. She saw the lights over the dunes, felt the ground shudder. For a second, she thought it was her own body and what Melanie was doing to her. Then she understood and let her head fall back onto the sand.

Dr. Das was okay, Earth 6 was not.

Earth 7, which Dr. Das didn’t know about, was safe in a boxcar in the sand.

Dr. Das and the surviving researchers drove away in a caravan, a line of vehicles sliding through the hills. Dylan was left in charge of the ruins.

19

There is time to wait. The water will come.

A single drop held together by its own internal gravity will resist the powerful pull of the planet for only so long. It will lose the battle, stretch, its meniscus ripping, and at last Earth will yank it to the ground. It will not splash but sink into the sand, where the tardigrades, a new desert species, wait to reconstitute once again.

Tardigrades. Known by the human world as waterbears because under the microscope they look like wiggly little bears. They are featured in movies and songs. Cutie-pies. A few dozen cells each, depending on the species. They'd make perfect pets (of course humans would think that way: mine), but tardigrades are loose and free. They've been crawling over every continent for half a billion years, through every disaster this planet has seen. They've been shattering into twelve hundred species. They've been rinsing off moss and plants and trees and into rivers in clumps. Millions of them riding on mud or swirling on leaves and branches. They are pushed down waterways on tides, along with the other microscopic animals, the minute members of the psammon—the rotifers, the nematodes, the gastrotrichs—all flowing into the drier areas, which are drying further, bit by bit, turning arid.

A hundred different tardigrade species washing up here in this desert. Arriving, encamping. Settling in.

Tardigrades passing through a thousand generations. Evolution is nothing to these creatures. They need only the tiniest drop of water to revive. They surge out of and sink into tun, waxing and waning, as the next drop comes and the one after that, until the miracle: a shower, fifteen minutes of falling water, so much that the little organisms are swimming—but tardigrades don't swim! Nearly drowning! Some drowning! Some surviving, holding fast to their giant grain of sand, weathering the storm, thriving, strengthening, multiplying. Then, in the long drought that follows, drying, nearly dying, many dying, some surviving, until the next drop dews into existence or falls from the sky, crashing, landing in the sand.

Voilà. A new species.

A new species clearly superior to those lazy, happy tardigrades of faraway lakes and rivers, those slow fatties, who waste an entire hour or two poking or getting poked in the stomach ("sex"), and who drag their eggs behind them in a sack like an anchor, eggs that take *two weeks* to gestate—who has the time?

The desert waterbears (sandbears?), meanwhile, achieve this and much more on a sped-up timeline. They are like arctic creatures, alien, inventive, can withstand anything Earth offers. Lesser tardigrades would goggle in surprise (tardigrades do have "eyes," two single photoreceptor cells) at these tough nieces.

Desert tardigrades come out of tun like Superman ripping off his glasses. They get busy immediately. They meet, fuck, have babies, *live*, in a matter of a day. And in their brief window of frantic, ecstatic activity, they feel all the joy and pain of any other creature. (Who's to say they don't?) Perhaps they feel it all the more, for they are aware of what is coming. They feel the *slow* approaching within the fast, the stasis within the kinetic, much as humans sometimes say they feel the presence of death in moments of joy. (The word for this experience is "awe.") Desire, wonder, fear—the desert tardigrades would say they know them all, or their own private Idaho of them.

And when tun arrives, most species of tardigrades (those weakling, watery, twice-removed cousins) are defeated after a few decades, while the hardy desert species knows how to sleep, knows the gifts of total temporary annihilation in a way that those who spend their lives "living" could never understand.

It is these tardigrades, the mighty sandbears, that a giant human scoops out of the sand and drops onto a watery slide. Soon they are coming out of tun. They are stretching, wobbling. Soon there are more of them, and more. A tremendous number. They are walking around on a film of water, rolling, eating whatever's there, filling up, hoping to meet someone special for a date before the day is out.

But they don't meet someone special. Instead, one by one they feel a poke, and not a good one! Something is squeezed into them, ouch! They do not know they are being saddled up for a long trip. The human with specialized tools is harnessing a backpack onto each of them, a molecular cuticle filled with DNA, a suitcase containing the future. The human inserts it inside them like a tumor. The human exclaims. Success! But for the tardigrades, it is not a success. There's an uncomfortable lump there! They can work around the lump. But already they are drying, slowing! It is too soon, they have not had their date! It has not been a good day, there is a lump. The lump can stay there while they sleep.

The last sensation they have—though at this point they are as close to being in full tun as a microscopic flake of dead skin—is of being gently nuzzled between grains of sand (or, to them, *home*). Return and arrival. Wait for revival. They tuck into the sand for a long sleep, their backpacks snuggled in their arms.

20

An actual road. Tar, paint, gravel. A sign on a pole in the concrete that read *Bus Stop.* Three Martians stood beside it. A straight line to the horizon in both directions. A muck of metals in the air. The Martians rotated their heads upward to examine the sign. They waited.

A faint buzzing. It was far off and so quiet it took them a while to notice. It grew louder in tiny increments and at last they could see it, a bright dot. It swelled into a squarish piece of silvery, humming alloy. It was hurtling toward them. It came on so fast that it might crash into them! It halted. *Company Bus* was printed across the top and *To the Future!* along the side. The Martians got on. It was empty. Bright green lettering scrolled around the walls. The buzzing started up again and the bus began to move, automated and coasting on solar power over company lands, heading to the edge of them and to the other side.

They were pursuing a lead. A final lead, Zee promised.

Decades of traces. Zee had been looking for traces for so long, he wasn't sure why anymore. He had been looking for most of his life. Mars wanted souvenirs. All the packaged food, clock radios, sleeper sofas, desk lamps he'd sent back. Prom dresses, puffy coats, any clothing, really, tutus, flannels, any utensils, any toys, any object at all, most of it broken, bent, expired, stained, didn't matter, as long as it was a trace. Fad plastics: Teflon, vinyl, forevers. Tinfoil twirled around cardboard. And rocks for the scientists. How the scientists loved rocks! Even gravel or dust. Sifting through the rubble, bagging up the leftovers of the lost planet. Shipping back load after load in container ships for the Martians to get bored with, so much trash that they'd begun their own dump on Mars. The great transfer. When Zee took the job on the trace team all those years ago, he'd thought Earth would be a trove, but of something else.

There'd been *one time*, his very first year in Earth orbit, when he'd seen a glimpse of what was possible. He'd connected with a child—a daughter living with her mother in a bubble below surface level. (The things Earthlings came up with: Why live like you were on Mars if you didn't have to?) He'd been lonely up in orbit, and the daughter was hilarious, adorable, fun. She chatted nonstop, swerved between topics, sent voice memos and videos. And she was sophisticated. Smart, you could not pull one over on her. God, she was gorgeous—untouched, undefeated, alive, so human. No artificial blah blah blah. All she wanted was to get out. He understood. He wanted out too. All she wanted was Earth. That's what he wanted too. He considered his feelings toward her similar to what one might have for a little sister. *Family love*, fascinating. You didn't really have that on Mars. Then she sent him a trace list, and he knew he was looking at an inventory of a different caliber. Molecular traces: animals and plants, thousands of them. She said she had the collection preserved for a future Earth. He was new, young, on his first mission. On Mars he'd lived in a hypermediated spacebox. He'd never been "outside" before, not really, not without enough protective equipment to sheath every millimeter of his body. He hadn't been to Earth's surface. He studied the list on his device and imagined his skin encountering air. He imagined taking off his helmet, breathing in the home planet. He showed the trace list to his superior.

"What makes you think she has all this? Earth is full of lists of things that no longer exist."

Zee pressed all emotion out of his face and said nothing.

His superior scratched his chin. "But if she *does* have them."

Zee held his breath.

"Could be interesting."

Zee allowed himself a nod.

He didn't yet hold rank to descend, so the trace team went without him. When they returned, his superior called him in. Zee could tell by his face that the mission had gone very, very wrong.

His superior was enraged. They'd been pranked, he said, by a child. It was obvious the moment they arrived that the traces could not be managed in that small space. Where were the freezers, the generators, the labs? Either a prank, or an attempt to lure them. A plot to steal the ship, journey to Mars, destroy the station, infiltrate Martian intelligence. (Here Zee nearly laughed—*what* intelligence?)

"Did you tell the daughter she was coming along with us?" his superior demanded.

Zee closed his eyes.

"Because she seemed convinced."

It was a professional disaster. His superiors reviewed all Zee's communications and were aghast. They revoked his privileges, rolled his merit points back to zero. They put Zee on a project studying dust. His job was to monitor atmospheric particles and their components—the same old, old questions about the origins of the universe.

He was devastated.

Those days! Trapped in the thermosphere with the orbital space trash, so much junk it was like swimming through a meteor shower. (He'd always been a little claustrophobic.) He was so unhappy.

But he didn't go back to Mars. He worked, he slept, he waited. And at certain moments, he'd look out at the blue atmosphere, at the particular configuration of stars from his vantage, the dead satellites crowding the live ones like sky ghosts, the peculiar molecules floating by, and he'd feel a sense of beauty and solitude that resembled peace. He'd pull up the daughter's list and scroll. Humans had wasted so much time searching for life in the universe, when all you could imagine had always been right here.

Four years later, he planted his boots on Earth's surface.

He stepped out onto a pile of rubble, took off his helmet, and breathed. It was glorious.

He coughed.

He walked on Earth, retrieved, packaged, sent into orbit all that was asked of him, and he took in every golden minute of it. It took a decade for disillusionment to set in. All the trash metals, trash plastics, concrete crumbling in his hands, useless fabric, whole continents of trees crushed into toilet paper and flushed into sewage. So depressing. He made it to the underwater bubbles where the daughter had once lived. The bubbles were in stasis now, empty of humans, full of artifacts. One bubble contained solely bars of gold, that old saw, it was almost cute. He tossed one into a bag. He had to admit his superiors were right. The traces could not have been here.

The trace crew shrank every year. The Martians up top were moving on to other projects. Some days Zee wandered the planet alone. He stuck to the deep desert, as far from the company's hold as he could get. He liked to move around the few populous areas, feel the buzz of Earthlings. Their posturing and bartering, their flirting. The refugees, the sand people. He was touched by their freedom, their free fall, their ceding. He tried not to think about the list, but it kept floating back into his consciousness. He hadn't understood how special that list was, that forevermore he'd be pulling out pieces of foam and rubber and glass melted into shapes. It nagged him. Maybe the traces did exist, not in the bubble, but somewhere, and the daughter knew where. Where had she gone? Maybe she was with them now. It was foolish but he couldn't let it go. He got into the habit of pulling up photos of her from long ago, asking around. Had anyone seen her? It wasn't unusual for someone to come by looking for a loved one. Earthlings looked at the photo, passed it around, said, "Sorry, no." He circled through the handful of oases. One in particular he liked. Rebel energy, a party in the sand. Seemed like the kind of place she would go. He was beginning to believe she was out there and that the molecular traces were too. "Do you know this person?" No one did.

In his dreams he dropped his devices, removed his trackers, left them in the sand, got on the company bus, disappeared into pop. Became Earthling.

By the time he rose in the ranks, waited out his turn, came to be captain, he was numb. The trace collection was an aging project, winding down. The crew had shrunk to the single digits, their ship swapped out for a craft so small the kitchen folded into the wall. He was promoted to captain by default—Command had never been more indifferent to him. Probably they hadn't given it much thought at all.

He poked his head into Recreation. His crew was playing video games and getting high. All they did these days.

"I'm going to tube down, check out a trace," he said.

Chuck paused the game and looked up.

Zee had only two crew members. Chuck and GlennB. They both hated him.

Zee stepped over to the tube. "Be back later."

Chuck unpaused the game.

He tubed down to the oasis. He hadn't been there in a while. Each visit, the place felt more and more like an encampment. Mostly deserted. Tents held down by cinder blocks, a few items laid out for sale on blankets. Universe dust coming through on the wind. He went from tent to tent, held out his device to Earthlings who looked dazed, zapped by solar rays, smothered by sand. "Has anyone seen this person?" She'd be a grown woman now, so he used a program to age her a little. Earthlings were less friendly these days, more suspicious, sicker, meaner. He went over to the bar and sat on a stool. A woman sat down beside him. He'd give it one more try. He dangled his device. "Have you seen this person?" She took the device in her hand, scrolled through the photos, watched a video. After a while, she said yes.

That night, Zee scooted back up to the ship, unzipped the tube, and stepped out. He was humming with energy. "She's alive," he said. "I think I know where she is."

"Who?" Neither Chuck nor GlennB bothered to look up. They were in a battle for their lives, shooting and spraying, pellets going everywhere.

"Command called," GlennB said.

Damn. After all these years, Command chose *this* moment. They were closing the project down, they said. A mission that had gone on so, so long. Martians had enough souvenirs. They were pulling the funding, taking away the spaceship, calling the team back. Zee and his crew were cleanup—as if they'd ever been anything else. The crew should prepare to leave orbit. Secure the ship. Sit tight in the thermosphere. The ship would auto-out on its own in a week. Command had already programmed the thing. Head home.

Zee's crew was elated and took a few minutes to cheer. Then they turned back to their game.

> ZEE: *Request permission to follow up on a final lead.*
>
> COMMAND: *Specify, Martian.*
>
> ZEE: *A cache of traces, a molecular collection.*
>
> COMMAND: *Negative. Storage shows your bins at capacity.*
>
> ZEE: *We'll throw away those rocking chairs. They don't even work on Mars.*
>
> COMMAND: *Negative.*

Zee poked his head into Recreation. "We'll take the ship down to the surface in six hours. Trace job."

Chuck paused the game and took off his headset. "Nah." His favorite word. "Command said to sit tight. We'll follow Command."

"I'm in command."

"Command's in command."

"We follow this final lead and we're out." Zee's hand lifted and became a vehicle whooshing through the air. "It's better than just sitting here."

"Nah."

Chuck, a journeyman, gaunt and haunted as a vet, constructed of sharp edges. His face was creased in verticals from an accident long ago. Zee had known him for many years. Pain in the ass for most of them, though they'd been friends once, or at least allies.

Zee straightened his shoulders. "Our mission is trace retrieval, Martian."

"We got enough traces." That was the other crew member, GlennB. Bald and lasered to a matte sheen, had the look of flexible plastic. He was just a kid on his first mission, subbed in last year (bad luck) and hating it.

"You just want to go back to Earth." Chuck made a kissy face. "You love Earth."

Zee did love Earth.

And he was captain.

They descended to the surface in a cascade of light and sound. They left the ship hidden in a pile of trash, on standby, ready for remote commands. "We can't fly this thing around on the surface, scare the Earthlings," said Zee. "We'll leave it far enough away that they can't track us coming. We'll call it when we're ready to load up."

"How are we supposed to get around without a ship?" said GlennB.

"We'll take the bus, you moron," said Chuck.

So they waited at the bus stop and got on.

They rode down highways, through tunnels, and over bridges. The bus was the cleanest, most efficient vehicle they'd seen on this planet. When they arrived at the end of the line, they stepped down, but they were sorry to see it go. The bus asked them to rate it. "A goddamn pleasure," said Chuck and smacked its chrome side. They walked off over a smooth platform of tar. GlennB tested its strength with his boots. "A landing area?" he said. "A stage?"

"Parking lot, B."

"Ah."

"Martian sees parking lot for the first time."

"All right, all right."

They found themselves in a desert town so bleached and

rubbed down, it looked like bones or ghosts or headstones or heaven. A battered sign lay in the sand. *Buy Organic.* A civilization of signs, instructions everywhere, a world endlessly explaining how to understand it. They stood in the particle-filled air with their gear. At last a truck trundled up and stopped. A dusty face in the window. "Where you headed?" the driver rasped. The Martians lifted their arms and pointed. "You got cash?" Zee held out his palm. The driver waved them to the back and they climbed in. They rode off into the desert. No pavement, no signs, no markings of any kind, just drifts.

They rode through fields of solar panels a hundred kilometers long, pieces of bent polymer, worn out and abandoned, sticking out of the ground like dried hides. They rode through a forest of steel, a monoculture of windmills, the giant blades dismantled and strewn on the ground like fallen leaves. They rode by the giant cannons that blew sulfur and diamonds into the air on an automated system replenished by robots. They passed through a million tonnes of carbon pulled out of the sky and left, like scattered boulders the size of cars.

The truck dropped them off in a spot that looked like nowhere but Zee had it pinned on his device. A little ways off was the one structure near the dump large enough to be the lab where the death cult had found the daughter. Zee had picked it up with radar. They walked, jangling in their bulky gear, through an onslaught of radioactive waves, their monitors pinging and beeping. At last, up ahead they spotted a pale construction.

"That's got to be it," said Zee.

They headed toward it. He was right. The lab facility was hanging in the air like a skeleton. The Martians stepped into its striped shadow. Its walls were down in jigsaw pieces, the concrete ripped from the iron frame.

They crunched through the grid. The giant silver tanks had

ruptured and rocketed through the wall. A few dozen of them. They'd landed like meteorites in the sand. Zee touched one, lifted his ashy finger to his tongue, and tasted. So this is it, he thought. Or was. He'd missed it. Again. Like so much on Earth.

"She's here," said Zee. "She's nearby."

"Nah," said Chuck.

The ruthless wind, the mash-up of sound, the untamed light, full of feral particles, the knot of Earth of which he himself was the thinnest thread.

"We don't have time for this," said Chuck. "The ship'll remote out in five days. I'm going to be on it."

"We've got time."

"It won't leave without us, will it?" said GlennB.

"I guarantee you, it will," said Chuck.

They kept walking. Late in the hot evening, they came across a sunken lake. On inspection the lake turned out to be an unbelievable number of birds, all the same bird, billions of them, their bodies liquidated with chemicals, along with their excrement, so not really a lake at all, but a sort of funereal goop. An Earth woman was sitting on the ground beside it. They handed her a container of filtered water and she folded her hands around it.

Zee asked her about the daughter. He crouched down beside her and showed her the photos.

"I'll tell you what I know, but it won't help," she said.

"It all adds."

"Sometimes her machine rides by in the night."

"Here?"

She took a long drink. "She's guarding the next Earth."

"This Earth?"

"She's dangerous. Be careful. She killed thirty people in the desert."

Chuck and GlennB exchanged looks.

"She went out into the sand and died and came back."

"I know about all that," said Zee. "Where does she live?"

The woman began coughing. Zee nodded at GlennB, who pulled out another bottle of water and gave it to her.

"Show me. I can pay you." He held out his device with the map shining on its screen.

She reached for it.

They had nowhere to sleep but Earth that night, so the Martians lay on the ground. Zee spread out like a snow angel and felt the precise grip of the planet holding him there. He listened to the low roar of the tectonic plates of a loose planet.

"Me? I had that much DNA, I'd make a park," said GlennB.

Chuck raised his head from the ground. "You mean like a safari?"

"Yeah," said GlennB, "but real, not VR." He maneuvered in his protective suit to sit up. "See, you're driving through the jungle, all terraform and beautiful. You round a corner and you spot—a rat! But real. A real rat."

"That's a farm," said Chuck.

GlennB made a sound that might have been a rat vocalization.

"On safari you saw, like, a bear."

GlennB ticktocked a finger. "Where would a bear walk on Mars? It would collapse, not enough density. Better a nice rat. Easy to build. Friendly, smart, big personality." He spread his arms. "I would build a rat's nest," he said expansively, "for the children to play."

"That is so idiotic," said Chuck. After a while, he added, "Besides, no one wants that DNA on Mars."

Zee blinked at the sky. He knew Chuck was right. Martians had moved on. It was out of fashion, way out of fashion, to construct a species with no habitat, let it enact a life variant in a cage variant until it died. It was freakish. Mars had hybrids if they wanted animals. Time to look ahead. Focus on the future—for *humans*, not chase a past they'd lost.

So why, Zee? Why are you still looking? Lost world, planet of your ancestors. You want it that badly? Quit being such a baby, Zee. Everyone lost out. Martians will always long for home. It's the human condition. Most never even got to see Earth. You got to spend decades on it, poking through the trash.

Yeah, but it was already broken by the time I saw it. I never saw it whole.

Get over it.

Zee watched the sky. The stars he had decided were stars, not satellites, were revealing themselves to be satellites, stealthily crawling across a meter of space, their orbits slowly degrading, trailing Earth as it spun and rotated and drifted away from the sun 1.5 centimeters per year. So many satellites, they hung from the top of the sky to the bottom, cascading down, brighter than stars, newer, updated from those ancients, less twinkly. But Zee preferred the ancients, those old fellows—dim, distant, dull in their shine and their predictability, stoic, unaffected by humans.

"How about you, Zee?" said Chuck. "What's your big dream?"

"Downsized so much it no longer exists," said Zee. "You?"

Chuck folded his arms behind his head. "I'm just ready to go home. Do something else."

Meanwhile, inside their jumpsuits, cells divided and divided and divided. Matter wafted through the air around them. Fragments of DNA, separated from their sources, floated on breezes, sticking to whatever they hit, the side of a space suit, a grain of sand, or they hit nothing and kept going, passed on by, receded into the night.

In the morning, they got another ride. They were close now, but not close enough to walk, so they sat in the back of a truck with some strays—humans and dogs. The air burned their lungs and their eyes. The Martians got out their masks, adjusted the levels, and sat back. They watched the dust storms in the distance, moving across the plain. Zee saw clearly now. He had the map with the Earth woman's mark on it, and he knew where he was going.

Earthlings. How rumpled they were, how defeated. But who doesn't love an underdog?

The Martians stumbled off the truck, fell, stood, straightened, limped. Headed toward the daughter.

21

Dylan waited. She let her eyes revolve around the room, over the insulation and wood paneling she had installed herself, over the card table. She and Melanie had dragged most of the furniture outside years ago. Some of it was lost, buried in the sand. The storage container itself was half lost, sand up to the window. A barchan would overtake the place in a decade. But she could still see out the window. Perhaps Melanie was sweeping the sand away every day. Only way in now was through the trapdoor in the ceiling, which was an ordeal for her in this condition. The underground room was intact, but she had no need of it anymore. Earth 7 was finished.

She looked out into the night. Shifting figures, shadowy forms. Maybe those were swaying trees, but, no, she must be confused. She had seen trees in her life, of course, but not many. She'd spent her childhood looking out at trees, dead underwater ones that broke apart in the water as she grew. A couple tree skeletons stood in the desert nearby. But swaying trees, like the ones she thought she was seeing? That was impossible here.

"Melanie," she said. She heard Melanie rustle somewhere behind her. "There's someone out there."

Melanie bent over and looked out. "No, I don't see anything."

Between the moving shadows she saw pieces of her own

reflection, a shiny rectangle of her shirt and neck, as if she were disappearing.

"Go look."

Dylan was waiting.

It had taken a while for Dylan to become sick. A decade of life in the container had gone by, and then the better part of another, before the illness even began, though really who knew when it began. Once it made itself known, it was ferocious and fast. She vomited into the garbage pail while Melanie was tapping on her improvised drums outside, a *Flintstones* rock band of one, humming, making up songs. Dylan was sweating. She vomited again, convulsed. She didn't notice the drums stop. Melanie was on the ladder.

Dylan wiped her mouth. "I'm not getting enough sleep."

A month went by. She didn't want Melanie to know it was getting worse, but she stumbled, dropped her plate, fell asleep on the floor on top of her food, woke, garbled, in pain, asking for her mother. Melanie tried to get her into a chair but she flopped over. Melanie pushed Dylan's damp hair away from her face, said, "We need help."

They hadn't heard from Dr. Das in a year, but Melanie sent him a memo. She wanted to bring Dylan in for treatment, she said. He sent a memo back within an hour and said no. He sent a memo again two days later and said yes. He asked for Dylan's location. Melanie didn't answer. He sent another memo. The last message wasn't from him, he said. People were getting into his account at the clinic. Don't bring Dylan. Listen, do *not* bring Dylan. He sent another memo an hour later and said, Of course bring Dylan. In fact, he'd come pick her up himself. Where was she? Give him the location. For some reason her location wasn't showing, which was a violation of company policy, as she knew. Melanie didn't answer. He sent another memo, said, Look, Dylan needs to be here, with us, where we can help her. There are experimental treatments. There are options. There are offers. Melanie played Dylan the memo. Dylan lifted her hand from the blanket and said wearily that she didn't want options or offers, especially not experimental ones. She'd be fine, she said, if she just rested a bit. And if not, what was so bad about dying? Happens to everyone. Or used to. She closed her eyes. He sent another memo and said there'd been a mix-up. That wasn't him who'd been writing. People were getting into his account again. This was the real Dr. Das. Dylan needed to answer. Dylan's brain was company property. It was in her mother's will. That had to be a lie, said Dylan. She wouldn't do that, would she? It was a trick. Dylan was sitting up at that point, arranged in the chair by the window.

"They killed him," she said, turning away. "They put him in the cloud."

Melanie disconnected the server. They stayed.

She was only forty-four—so what was wrong with her? Maybe it was the contamination, the radiation. Or maybe she'd inhaled too many years of sand. Maybe she'd lived in the ocean too long, while her bones and synapses and systems were still developing. Artificial air, artificial sunlight, pseudofood made of chemicals, a human raised in a cage, it would have to catch up with you.

Meanwhile, Melanie was heartier than ever, went for long walks deep in the night while Dylan slept, played her drums till dawn. Her face was drooping a bit more on one side these days, but she could kind of clip it in place.

Dylan, still at the window. "Go look, Melanie, would you? Someone's there. Or coming." She felt sure of it. Melanie rustled, relented.

She clinked up the ladder, disappeared. Dylan waited. Was the window already covered by sand and Dylan was looking at nothing? Was she hallucinating? She wasn't sure.

She heard the trapdoor lift, the scrape and squeak of it. Melanie was coming back. Someone was with her. She heard voices. If it was the company, well, she'd rather just die right now.

A man was in front of her. "Zee," she said. She knew him immediately. As symmetrical as ever, he stood in a shiny yellow outfit. "You came."

"I did." He knelt beside her.

"You took a while."

"Yes, sorry."

"I made it out."

Zee smiled. "Sort of," he said, looking around.

"Got to live somewhere."

He laughed a little. He had aged too.

"Did you see my mother out there anywhere?"

"I'm afraid not."

"Ah." She waved a hand and let it drop. "Tell me," she said. "Still hunting traces?"

He brightened, raised his device. "I kept your file. This is our last stop."

She reached out a shaky finger and touched the screen, scrolled. "It's all there, or at least the good stuff is. I saved it for you."

22

When Zee and his crew arrived at the home of the daughter Dylan Stein, landed their spacecraft in the boulders and dust, the first thought they all had was: *Mars*. They'd been to plenty of places that held a similar backdrop, of course, but this spot in particular resembled one where ships left and landed on that planet.

Mars, they thought. *Home*.

For one of them, the two words arrived in his mind as equivalents, *Mars* = *home*, and whatever emotions that dragged in (yearning, repulsion).

For another, the second word came as a question, *Home*? As in: I have just seen Mars in my mind and realized I do not think of it as home, so where is my home?

For another, the two words were separate, unconnected thoughts: This place looks like Mars. And after that thought had broken up and dispersed into the ether, the next thought arrived: *Home*. Because *home* is what Zee thought every time he looked at Earth.

Home, that elusive place, they thought. How many years have I spent trying to shake it off? How many years trying to get it back?

They had their spaceship. They had summoned it from the garbage pile. It had lifted, turned in the air, and flown to them. But the abracadabra of it all had taken longer than Zee expected, and now they had only thirty hours until the ship would heave into orbit and shoot off for Mars, with or without its humanish cargo. They would need to be fast.

"All right," said Chuck. "Where is she?"

"Right behind us. Over that ridge."

The air was orange with particles.

They assembled and began walking. But a figure was already waiting for them on the ridge. They hailed her but she didn't answer. Could it be the daughter come to meet them? The Martians had on their oxygen packs and night goggles, but the figure had on only a paper mask and a cloak. There was a bit of wind. They approached clunkily, sliding in the sand. The figure lowered her hood. It was an Earth woman, or an approximation of one, but certainly not the daughter. Zee removed his mask and so did she. "We are on a mission from Mars," he said. "We've come to speak with the daughter Dylan Stein."

"Mars," the Earth woman said. "That's cute."

Zee felt a sinking in his chest. Another person to get through, and they had so little time. "Who are you?" he said.

"The wife." She folded her arms.

After a while Chuck took off his mask. "It looks like you've been modified."

"Yes."

"May I ask for what?"

"Eternal life."

Something moved over her face as she said it, and Zee felt compelled to reassure her. "Don't worry, it won't work," he said, though really he had no idea.

Sand blew across their legs in the low wind. They'd been standing only a few minutes and already their boots were sinking. How could the daughter keep the traces here with all this sand? They'd be buried. For the first time he had doubts.

“As the wife, you could grant me an audience.”

“I could,” said the Earth woman, “but I won’t. Dylan does not want to be uploaded. You can take your companymen and go.”

Zee sighed. What was the Earth woman talking about? He had never really gotten his head around the company. There were no companies on Mars, and the idea of them seemed garish. How was he going to get the Earth woman to help them? Earth women were so mean. They did not even respect the Martian nonviolence code. Martians had been shoved by Earth women. They’d had things thrown at them. The Martians could try to use their sensory equipment to search for the traces, but that would take too much time. The desert was huge. His crew was so tired. His lungs ached. They were on a clock. Beside him, Chuck and GlennB were silent, sucking in and out through their oxygen masks.

He pulled himself up. “I don’t know about companymen, Earth woman. We’re here on official business. Escort us.”

She laughed and pulled up her hood. She began to walk away.

Zee was desperate. He called out to her: “My name is Zee.” She stopped. That was enough for him to continue. “The daughter once lived in the ocean on a kilometer of calcium carbonate. That is when I knew her. I don’t have much time and I’ve come a long way.”

She turned around.

“Please. I believe she would want to see me.”

The Earth woman stepped toward him. “She’s sick.”

“How bad?”

“Soon I’ll be a widow.”

He was crushed, though he had no right to be.

“Follow me,” she said.

They followed the Earth woman to a large crate lodged in the sand. She pointed to a porthole so small that Zee had to remove first his air tank, then his helmet, then his boots. Finally he stripped down to nothing but his reflective jumpsuit and he stepped in, crawled down the ladder on his own. There she was.

She was much diminished, thinned out and flattened. Zee couldn't believe how old she looked, but she gave him a wide smile, and beneath the age he could see her as he knew her from the photos and videos. Her mind was still clear and she welcomed him like an old friend. He was very glad to see her. "You took a while to get here," she said. She asked him about her mother, but Zee didn't know where she was. And sure enough, all these years, she'd kept the traces safe. She was happy it was him, she said. "Could you get my device?" she said to the future widow. She transferred the coordinates to him and told him how to break the code the coordinates were in. He wondered where there could be such a facility out here, generating the power to preserve all those traces. She said not to worry. "But who is taking care of them?" he said.

"No one."

He had so many questions, but time was going by fast. His crew was waiting. He stood. The future widow stood too.

"I'd like to come along," she said. "As the wife, it is my right."

Zee hesitated.

"Take her," said the daughter. "The collection is hers when I die. So really it is her gift to give."

Martians did not believe in that category of ownership—inheritance—but Zee said quickly, "We'll bring you, of course. Come along."

They got the hover and its storage trailer out of the ship and the three Martians got in, along with the future widow.

They skimmed over the sand. They were farther out than Zee had ever been, riding through a slay of particles from old wars, radioactive rays with half-lives of tens of thousands of years, along with other kinds of radiation incompatible with life. Their sensors were beeping and flashing. It didn't take long to understand what had happened to the daughter. This was no place for human habitation, but the Martians kept quiet and Zee turned off the sensors.

At last the hover stopped. They'd arrived. Inside, the air filters and cooler churned.

"Where is it?" said Zee.

"Underneath," said the widow.

It just looked like a sand dune, like anything hidden below must have been there a hundred years. Where were the building, the generators?

"You sure?" said GlennB. He was leaning forward between them to check the location screen.

The future widow looked on. "It's there."

They got out.

They dug. They were slow because of the sand, which poured in as it came out, but they had equipment to help with this. They had all the tech: instruments to listen to the ground and reveal the shape of what was below, instruments to measure how densely the sand was packed, where the sand ended and another substance began. It took quite a while. They had the coordinates punched into the magnetic box but the traces had shifted in the sand. They had to dig farther. At one point it moved—they had destabilized it (GlennB's fault). They had to rearrange their equipment, move it all half a meter to the left, and go slower. Then a reading came in and they scrambled as close to the hole as they dared. Not much later they were looking at a plate of metal. They'd found it.

They cleared away more sand. The area was large enough to be a rectangular room. "Yes, that's it," said the widow. She'd come over to have a look. "It's an old boxcar."

Zee frowned. There would be an alarm system to trigger drones or weapons. How Earthlings loved alarm systems! The Martians would have to disable it. He asked the future widow, but she said there wasn't one. She got back into the hover. Zee waved to his crew and the Martians huddled to discuss it. The Earth woman must be tricking them. She was going to blow them all to smithereens or trigger an avalanche and bury them. They spent a long time looking carefully but couldn't find one. Why wouldn't the daughter have secured it? Zee was surprised enough that he called the operation to a halt to think. They stood outside, staring down at the boxcar in the sand. The widow wandered over and stood beside them.

Eventually she spoke. "How long have you been collecting traces?"

"I've spent my life following leads," Zee said.

Chuck groaned. "Nobody wants to hear about your rotten childhood."

They all looked down at the boxcar.

"What's Mars like?" she said.

"It's not what you think," said GlennB.

"It's dark," said Chuck. "Everybody lives underground."

They'd been asked this before.

"What are you going to do with all this stuff?"

"We're just the retrieval team."

They'd been asked that too.

"Will you take us with you?" she said.

They'd been asked that too.

At last they agreed: The daughter had not secured it. They prepared to continue.

By the time Zee strapped on the pulley, it was nearly dawn. The ship would be leaving in six hours. The future widow was standing back, her hair gray and thick, flying to the side in the stiff wind. Her face glowed a dim neon. Zee dropped down onto the roof in the slip attached to the pulley, his feet touching the old wood as gently as possible. He braced himself for a fall or an explosion. His weight alone could cause an avalanche. Then Chuck came down, too, and they waited a moment before letting go of the ropes. They worked at the vent. It had been boarded up and sealed tight. They wrenched it open and Zee went through, leaving the wind and entering the silent, cool, dark space. Chuck followed. It was indeed an old train car. They pointed their flashlights around.

On a low platform was a large rock—just a rock? They shone their flashlights at it. An ordinary boulder, like the ones scattered all over the universe, across a million planets. Zee brought his light closer and saw that there was a large marking on the top that read:

Just add water.

He switched his device to magnifying mode and studied it. He realized what he was looking at and felt the breath leave his body. She did it, he thought. "Look," he said. Etched all along the sides were minuscule markings, intricate drawings, lists, instructions, explanations, charts.

"Now, this seems a bit optimistic," said Chuck.

It was the most beautiful Earth trace any Martian had ever seen.

"Humans will do any stupid thing," said Chuck.

They each took a side and hefted it, inched it slowly across the room. Up top, GlennB lowered the pulley. They placed the trace inside the slip. "Careful," Zee called up. "Don't drop it." It would be like GlennB to drop it. Zee watched it rise out of sight. The pulley lowered again and Chuck went up. Zee was alone. He waited.

Was he really going back to Mars? He'd rather die than go back to that cold wasteland where you lived on VR and air constructed in a lab. He wanted Earth. It had always only been Earth for him. He didn't care if it was broken. He tapped his booted foot. One hard jump would destabilize this container. It could sink, it could take hours for Chuck and GlennB to dig him out. Hours they didn't have if they wanted to be on that ship auto-flying out. They'd leave him there. He was ready for that. Die, or somehow survive and stay. They'd take the trace rock back to Mars, where it would be safe.

But what if Chuck decided to dig him out? A sudden sentimental change of heart. Zee could see it, the asshole. Chuck, giving it all he had, saving Zee from the sand. The ship would leave without them and the trace would remain on Earth.

The pulley lowered and Zee grabbed it.

23

The Final Flight of Martian Zee

So he lost Earth, but also he had it, the last copy. They dropped the future widow off, waved goodbye, hurried to the ship with minutes to spare. He locked the Earth copy in a compartment, double secured—they would have to wrench the door away to get it out. As they blasted off and rocketed out of the atmosphere, Zee, strapped in, watched the mangled original itself getting smaller out the window.

The light was changing fast as they passed back through the stratosphere, lifted away from the homeland. The orb of Earth shrank, but he knew he had it with him—or the possibility of it. True, there were still so many steps between here and there to reach it, but at least he saw a path where before there was only blur. Out of this mission, because of him, the Martians of human descent could re-create the home planet. Somewhere, somehow. All they had been missing they could have once again and do it right this time.

But even as he thought it, he knew it would never happen. Chuck was right. It was impossible. He sank back, and they floated away from the one true Earth. Still, he imagined it, he imagined the impossible, what it could be. He imagined a thousand kilometers of forest, another thousand of tundra, another of living sea. He imagined all that might fill them, the life and the death, he imagined the churning cycle, life adding, expanding, evolving. He saw it and he slept.

24

"We're about at the end here."

"I guess so," said Melanie.

She and Melanie were sleeping outside on the desert floor, since she couldn't make it in and out of the container anymore. The same old lawn-chair recliners. Melanie arranged them in the shade of the container and set up the reflector over Dylan during the hottest part of the day, while Melanie spent a few hours inside the container in the cool. At night Melanie slept on the other chair beside her. They pulled sheets over their faces when the sand blew across them in blasts. Dylan lay very still as her body slowly destroyed. She was not unhappy, unless she thought of Melanie being alone.

In the final days she regretted nothing. Her mother. Maybe that. Dylan hadn't received the promised letters.

"Maybe she had nothing to say," said Dylan.

"What horseshit," said Melanie. "There were never any letters coming."

But Dylan had no anger anymore. Her mother had made Dylan the person she was and had given her a life's project, then had freed her by leaving.

A thought at the end: Earth itself would preserve what was best for it and leave behind what was worst. Whatever Earth came up with next would be perfect. There was no need of Earth 7 at all.

So Dylan died. Could she still see Melanie? Did Melanie appear, drifting above her, a bit out of focus, wavy, like seeing through water? Melanie faded. Dylan watched every last bit of light and color go out.

When Melanie was certain it was over, she got up and walked off, left even her solar bike. She walked a long way because what reason did she have to stay? She could keep going and going. But after half a night, she turned around and went back.

4

Earth, After

25

"Tell me about the night with the aliens," said Cami.

"They weren't aliens," Melanie said. "They were humans. The humans who left on the Mars mission long ago. The descendants, they survived."

The pale light was wisping over them. Sand blew onto the cot and was sticking to their thighs and butt cheeks.

"How do you know?"

"They told me."

"They were lying."

"No."

"Did they hurt you?" Cami rose on her elbows, frowning, her smooth face shining. "If they hurt you, why, I'll . . ."

"No, they were very polite," Melanie soothed.

This girl. Nothing like Dylan.

The light around them was growing stronger, the satellites blinking out. The dunes smelled of ancient ocean. They were naked under the sheet.

"Tell me what happened."

"I don't want you to get upset."

"Why would I get upset?" Cami kicked at the sheet and it fell off the cot, caught in the titanium legs. Melanie considered the girl's luscious thighs. Once Melanie told, Cami would disappear.

Worse, Melanie might be detained. Even if she ran, the company might come after her. It was nice to pretend.

"They wanted some DNA is all."

"They wanted to *clone* you?" Cami cried.

"They were here to excavate."

"Dead bodies?"

"They were looking for one of those old molecular collections. Used to be one here, a big facility." Though of course Cami knew that.

The sun was touching their toes, crawling up the cot, coming down the line of dunes that encircled them like giant ocean waves, a sea of sand, and she and Cami were adrift in it. Maybe all matter, all existence, is waves, she thought. Water, light, air, sound. The self itself a little tangle of waves, brain waves, waves of atoms and whatever is smaller than atoms. There was a theory that went like that—what was it called again? Dylan had said it had been unstrung, debunked, but replaced with what?

"What did you tell them?"

"The truth. I said, 'Oh, that place was ransacked so many years ago, nothing but rubble over there.'"

"What did they say?"

"They said, 'Yeah? Well, there's another. Hidden in the sand.' And I said, 'If there was, it's probably gone too.'"

Cami shifted onto her hip and was very quiet. "How did you know there was a collection here?'

Melanie lay back. "Come on, you know I was with someone who worked for the lab." She grinned. "I had a thing going with the groundskeeper." She reached over and twirled a lock of Cami's hair. She felt a pulse between her legs. "How'd you get so sexy?" She inched a hand over to that magnificent hip. "They teach you that in training?"

Cami laughed and leaned in, traced the contours of the

Regenerator. She loved Melanie's implants, said they were cool and beautiful, said she was going to get a head full of them, too, once her rotation was over. Cami was so young. Depop was history, something to be nonchalant about. The world had always been empty to this creature. Melanie herself barely remembered depop, though she'd been a child in the second wave and it had shaped her life. She had run from it for so long, until Dylan had grabbed her arm and stopped her.

Cami stopped kissing Melanie and pulled back. "How did you know about the other collection? The hidden one?"

"I didn't." Melanie squinted. She knew Cami was spying on her, and she was fairly certain it was for the company. Where could she even be hiding a recording device? She was completely naked. Melanie turned onto her back and blocked the sun with her arms. "I told them there couldn't be. That if there was one, the sands had surely shifted so much, it would be buried. But they wouldn't listen. They wanted to try. It was their mission. So I gathered some tools."

Cami's face was arranged with care. "Wait, why did they come to you? Why did you have to go with them?"

"They didn't, I didn't. I saw them come down. They dropped into the old oil field. I walked across the rocks and watched them get out."

"But you just said—"

That wasn't what happened. They'd landed in the rock pile behind the container where she'd been living peacefully with Dylan for so long. She'd gone out with a pair of binoculars as they approached. They called to her, broadcasting through a speaker from deep inside their helmets. They asked for Dylan Stein. She figured it was companymen, come to take Dylan away, upload her brain, toss her body into a furnace, like Dylan had always predicted. Or maybe it was rebels, come to destroy Earth 7, like Dylan had always feared. Or maybe it was Dylan's mother, returned from outer space, like Dylan had always hoped.

But then one of them took off his breathing mask and spoke. At first Melanie was unmoved, but then he said his name, and she remembered it from Dylan's stories. She stopped to listen. What he said made her think of that night with the cards, when she herself was crossing a great divide, not as wide as his, a divide mostly in her mind, but wide, and she had not known the reverberations her crossing would make. She'd looked at the stranger and thought: That trip across the sand on the cement mixer was the most glorious ride of my life. She decided to trust him.

Dylan died. That was the thing she hadn't counted on. Melanie could imagine leaving Dylan, had imagined it, had imagined Dylan leaving her, or making her leave—because of her age or the implosion or explosion of her face (still neither had happened), or because they'd gotten sick of each other. Melanie had forgotten about death. What do you do if someone dies? It's not that they stop reaching for you in bed or having long conversations with you about nothing. What if they get sick and die, your young wife, forty years your junior, your girl?

After she died, after Melanie walked away in astonishment and came back, she arranged Dylan's body on a blanket. She pulled her across the sand, out of the line of the approaching barchan, and towed her up a low dune. She buried her beside the old rowboat they used to sit in, and she constructed a path of white rocks leading to the grave. Then she just stood outside, let rage and grief wash over her. Nothing else to do. The sand-wind stung her face, made its sound-notes as it tapped. She felt her body changing the wind's course by being in its way, she felt her own participation in the wind's history. She tried to recall *Celebrity Plastics*. Who was Melanie before she let herself love Dylan? That old self was far away and she couldn't believe how lost that person had been. Why? It seemed ridiculous now. Really, she had Dylan to thank for being able to live without her, for not coming to pieces. That's what Dylan had given her: wisdom and death.

She stayed in the desert. She took long walks at dawn. The ground was full of bones. She wore an orange vest and a company hat when she went for supplies so the drones would know who she was. But many people slipped through undetected. Some passed by the container without stopping. She heard them rustle by in the dark in small groups. The sand people. Sometimes they stopped and asked for small assistances—to charge a battery or refill a water jug. She always gave, though she knew it wasn't a good idea, because that's how you got a reputation, and soon hundreds would be stopping by on their way and she'd be caught and charged. It was against company policy to help the sand people, since they might be rebels destroying infrastructure. Still, she gave.

Who knew, maybe one day she'd leave with one of them, disappear with only her backpack.

They came and went, and sometimes she slept with one, but so far she'd stayed. She had an odd sensation of waiting. She wondered if she would die. She hoped so.

Sand. She was really in it now. The thing about living in sand is the tremendous gathering of it, how it seeps under every lid that you know you screwed down tight, into every bag you carefully sealed. It is in the corners of your screens, in your food, your water, your clothes. It is embedded in your ears, and when you scratch your head it falls out of your hair. When the wind comes, it is in your eyes. If you are asleep, you wake blinking, blind, reaching for the "dead water," water too contaminated to drink but that can be used to splash on sand-coated eyes or to dab on your wrists and neck and forehead, the bottoms of your feet against the heat. The sand is trying to cover you, and it will succeed. It gathers by the door, piles against it, waits. If it wants to come in, it will, in small drifts, then large ones. If it wants to bury your home, it will. If it wants to bury you, it will. It is a moving animal, its legs are the wind. You can try to make a run for it, but it will find you.

Melanie remained. Talking to the sky, caretaking no one, groundskeeping nothing. Then out of nowhere came Cami, driving across the sand in her company security jeep, roaring up, saying she needed to check something out. Routine. She got out, sex streaming off her in ribbons. The way things went that first night, Melanie figured that at her age, she still had it.

But soon she understood the situation.

Still, Cami didn't arrest her that night or the next, didn't bring her in for questioning. Three weeks of visits passed. Maybe Cami's superiors thought they could get more information this way. She allowed herself to wonder if Cami was protecting her.

Either way, Melanie appreciated the distraction.

"What did they look like?" said Cami.

"Who?" Melanie dragged her mind back.

"The aliens!"

"Humans. I told you. They were human. They had on helmets so it was hard to see their faces. They had on contamination suits and breathing equipment. They had sensors wrapped around them and instruments attached, so it was hard to see their bodies. Their voices came out mechanical. But then one took off his helmet and you could see right away they were just people. 'Who are you?' I said, and they told me why they'd come. I asked if I could go with them."

"To Mars?" Cami demanded.

Melanie sighed. Poor Cami, the little kitten, a terrible spy, but also an envious girlfriend and a sucker for adventure. That part seemed real.

"No, silly. To look for the collection."

But, yes, later that night, she *had* asked to go to Mars. Could they take Dylan and her both? The Martians had said no.

"Did they torture you?" said Cami.

"Who?"

"For the information?"

"I didn't have any information."

"Then why did you go with them?" Cami shook her head. "It makes no sense. Why would they take you along if not for the information?"

Melanie sat up on an elbow. "Maybe they thought I could be of use. There might be things they didn't understand." She grinned slyly. "On any mission it's good to have a native civilian along."

"*I* told you that," Cami said miserably. "You're just quoting me. I learned that in combat."

Melanie reached over and patted her leg.

Cami sat up and looked out over the dunes. "What did you see out there?" She sounded wistful.

Melanie smiled. Cami hadn't been past the garbage. The shifting sands were dangerous and the company forbade the trip. Cami was brave and would have liked the adventure—so unlike Dylan. But she didn't like to disobey rules—also unlike Dylan.

"Nothing," Melanie said. "It was dark. I saw nothing at all."

She'd seen graveyards of rocks, the rubble of former villages, bleached adobe houses, outpost dwellings that might hold people still. She'd seen sand washes, rivers of sand through the sand. She and Dylan had spent years roaming them.

The hot air screaming by, the pale colors. Drying eyes.

Now and then the hover had stopped and the Martians got out, pointed their devices. Melanie didn't ask what they were doing. They'd exchange a few words on private channels she couldn't hear or in a language she didn't know. Then they'd climb back in and keep going. They had punched into their system the coordinates Dylan had given them, but that didn't seem to be the only method they were using.

"Did they let you drive?" said Cami.

She frowned. "Drive?"

"The hover. Did they give you a chance to do manual?"

"I don't believe anyone did manual."

Cami smirked and hugged her knees. "I bet they would've let me."

"No."

"Did you ask? They would've let me if I'd asked."

This kid. She needed to hear it, how it all went down, how she had missed out. That was the story for her in the end: She wasn't there, she didn't get to see beyond the garbage, didn't get to drive the hover, didn't get to dig to the bottom of the sand.

"So what happened next?"

"They found the spot and they dug."

"The Martians dug?"

"Well, no. We watched a robot dig. It took a long time. It was like digging out the body of the sphinx."

"The what?"

"Never mind. They got what they wanted."

"It was just sitting there?"

"Pretty much."

"And then?"

"They left."

"Where did they go?"

Melanie lay back. "Home, I suppose."

She'd told it all now. She'd need to leave fast, before she was arrested. But she didn't leave, and no one came for her. Not even Cami. A day went by. A week, a month. So perhaps Cami had protected her after all.

26

But Melanie received another visit. It was a decade later. No, two. She was old now, really old, and alone in that windy place with the satellites and the moon moving around overhead. She survived on so little, it hardly seemed possible, and indeed it wasn't possible—death was catching up with her, she could feel it. She was growing thin. Her face was shrunken around the implants and the Regenerator, which was still motoring away. She looked skeletal, mechanical. Each night she climbed out of the storage container through the trapdoor in the ceiling and slid down the sand. She lay outside on the lawn-chair recliner and watched the satellites watching her back.

One night she noticed one of the satellites growing larger. It was expanding. No, it was moving closer. It came out of the sky, lowered to Earth, and hovered above her. She could see its exterior silver plates. It was right over her head, buzzing. It dropped to the ground with a clank, landed beside her. It unfolded itself and straightened. There, in the night light, it was about the size of a refrigerator, shiny and metallic.

A real-life robot. Here! Not a fake human robot. Lights blinking, motor whirring. Whisps of smoke or ozone were floating off it and dispersing.

"What do you want?" said Melanie. "You're from the company, right? Come to take me away?" She took a few steps backward.

A panel on its top flipped open. Inside, a roller began to spin. A smooth voice emerged from a speaker she couldn't see. "This device," it said, "has been sent to the last known location of the genetic material of human Dylan Stein."

"Oh, that," she said with relief.

"I am to relay a message to human Dylan Stein."

"Yeah, she's gone. Decades ago. If you're here for the DNA or traces or whatever you want to call it, you missed that by decades too. That's probably a zoo on Mars by now."

"I am to relay a message to human Dylan Stein."

"Too late. I buried her in the sand."

The lights spun again.

"You buried her," said the robot, "as a punishment?"

"No."

"As a legal remedy?"

"No."

"Are you her enemy?"

Melanie sighed. "She was dead. Nonfunctioning."

The lights spun again.

"Are you her speaking agent?"

She thought about that for a while. "Yes."

"Speaking agent, I am to relay a message to human Dylan Stein."

"Who's sending this message?"

"Microchip 8A-28049RT."

"What's that?"

"Microchip 8A-28049RT corresponds to human Rosemary Stein."

"Her mother?" Melanie shifted to her other hip and frowned. "What took you so long?"

The lights spun. "Bring me to the genetic material of human Dylan Stein."

She waved an arm. "All right, let's go."

It wasn't far, but Melanie walked slowly these days. She was stiff and no longer had perfect balance. They went, she creeping, the robot rolling behind her, across a flat valley and up the low dune to the old rowboat she and Dylan had found and dragged to the only mesquite tree for miles around, dead but still standing. She stopped.

"Hey, Dylan," she said. "Your mother's here. Sort of." She turned to the robot. "She's there." She pointed to the sand.

"I will now deliver the message."

"Go ahead."

A hinge opened on the robot, almost like a jaw.

Melanie sat on the edge of the boat and waited. It was getting late and the satellites were rushing and retreating in their usual patterns, tracking and compiling, bouncing information across the sky, wind moving between them, the wind itself carrying its own heavy equipment of metals and matter.

The robot began.

"My dearest Dylan, I've left at last. After being stuck fast to a spinning rock for so long, I've wrenched free and hurtled into space. Thus far, it has been quite the journey. In the first seconds, I saw the Moon. It was zipping toward me with such speed, I was sure I'd crash into it, my adventure stymied seconds in by some minuscule miscalculation, and I'd be doomed to circle Earth listlessly forever. But I could barely form that thought before I shot by effortlessly. The Moon was long behind me. 'Faster than thought. Nice,' I noted in the log. Soon the sun itself was retreating. It was like going backward into a tunnel. Light was a large circle that kept shrinking until the sun resembled what it is: a star.

"I have great hopes for this trip. I've reviewed all the manuals, specs, and coding. I've been promised near-instantaneous transmission of letters. The transmissions will slow as I move farther away from Earth, of course, but it will be a long time before I can't send any at all. I imagine you receiving this and hearing a simulation of my voice. I imagine you at work right now, sweeping sand or putting away equipment in the shed, turning an idea over in your mind, looking up, thinking hello.

"What I have for you: a few words from afar. Some advice. Theories. I will try not to bore you with science or tech . . ."

The voice faded out into a static drone, and Melanie got up and gave the robot a whack on its side. It didn't help, but the voice slowly returned.

". . . and I've passed three stars so far. Two were very far from me and bright. I went by quickly—or they did—like giant diamonds rolling by. The third had the hard, dim glow of a rumbling furnace. Not that you've ever seen a furnace, but allow me to explain the star's mechanics . . ."

The robot went on. Melanie perched on the lip of the rowboat. Her mind began to wander. After a while, she sank back and stretched her legs over the planks. She watched the sky and the robot towering over her.

"Now I'm 'between spaces,' Dylan. That's what the company calls my state. I've left the last star behind and am heading to the next thing—a dark cloud that may contain particles of interest. The space I roam through is considered 'between' the last space and the next one, as if it were not space itself, which I assure you it is.

"I'll be here for some time, apparently.

"Of course, everyone is always between spaces. The only space you are not between is the one you inhabit. But do I inhabit space? I ride in a vehicle that inhabits space, but I am not a body anymore. My location is purely theoretical. So what am I between? I think about this. My mind without its body hums on, as ever. I have plenty of time to think."

Melanie yawned.

"Some instructions, Dylan, as regards the collection and your efforts with sand." Here Melanie zoned out, since there was nothing she could possibly do about it now, and she didn't want to hear about it.

The robot droned on and on. Melanie tuned in for the more human-seeming parts, like when she confessed, "I do miss sunrises. I miss even the word 'sunrise.' To think of those optimistic early humans, first forming words as they rode blithely on their rotating planet, believing their star was going 'up,' to believe in 'up' at all, to believe it for so long that, even after they knew better, still insisting on it, doubling down, *sunrise*, *sunrise*.

"I used to be so impatient with words that stand in for our errors, misunderstandings, haphazard guesses, as does so much of our language, but now I like it. Words are just a record of our ongoing bewilderment about what's around us."

The robot went on so long, Melanie grew sleepy and curled up in the rowboat, meaning only to rest, not meaning to miss it, wanting to show respect for a mother, even a bad one, and for a message that had traveled so far. But, alas, she wasn't able to give Dylan's mother her due. Ah, mothers! Poor, suffering mothers. It's so unfair. She fell asleep thinking about that, woke to hear the robot say, "Remember that, Dylan," but missed what it was that a dead woman shouldn't forget. She dozed again, woke with a start to the robot singing an old, old song. "The company bus goes round and round, round and round, round and round . . . Do you remember that, Dylan?" Melanie did remember it from her own childhood, and she murmured assent, mouthed a verse, then fell back asleep.

She woke again in the night feeling the robot's warm hum, its tinny voice still emerging from its fiberglass jaw. "Good night, Dylan, if that's what it is. I'm imagining you sleeping. Remember when we used to make artificial day and night in the pod? I tried to make things normal for you, though, as you know, I myself never saw much use in the division of time. Now even less so, when the rules of time I experienced and was taught turned out to be so small and limited and Earthbound. Consider: If time, the concept of it and all its applications, can be so easily upended, Dylan, think of all that can be toppled—our conception of life, our beliefs about existence, matter, personhood . . ."

Melanie was lying in the sand now. When had she gotten out of the boat?

"It's hard to explain . . ." the robot was saying.

She wasn't sure if she was dreaming or listening. "It *is* hard to explain," she said and drifted off again.

She was still listening as day broke. She lay there all morning in the shade of the boat, but as the sand heated up, she interrupted.

"Hey, I can't be outside this time of day. Could you stop for a while? Say, five or six hours?"

The robot paused but didn't respond. Then it went on.

"Hey, I'm the speaking agent. I command you to stop and wait until I return."

The robot paused and whirred, then kept going, something about atoms and their movements. "We never understood this, Dylan, until it was too late . . ." Melanie sighed and heaved herself to her feet. She went back down the dune and into the storage container and waited. She took a long nap, rose, and looked out the window. The robot was still there. She ate. She waited. She went out again as the sun began to dip toward the west horizon. She carried water and a lawn-chair recliner with her, though it was awkward and it took a long time. Before she made it to the top of the dune, she could hear the robot still spewing out its message, its long song.

"... and it is the company's solemn hope that millions more will follow my lead, and that the next step for humans will be a space civilization of freedom and inquiry."

"How depressing," mumbled Melanie. She dropped the chair into the sand. "Dylan would hate that, you know," she told the robot. "That's the problem with you people. No coherent vision. Are you making a zoo or putting everyone on chips? Make up your mind."

"Perhaps I'll run into you somewhere out here, Dylan, though the chances of that are low, indistinguishable from zero. And how would we know each other?"

"Should have thought of that before you left," said Melanie.

"I'm afraid I have calculated that, with my current distance, instantaneous transmission is impossible. It won't be long before I go beyond all reach of Earth and will be unable to send you messages."

Melanie stretched out on the chair. "Ah, that's better."

"I wish to say that I'm not sure I was entirely honest or forthcoming with you about my research. I retreated into letters. I want to apologize for that."

"A little late," said Melanie.

"The truth is, escape from Earth had always been the plan, or at least the dream—since I was a child. I didn't feel an attachment to Earth. I always believed I would feel more at home out here, and I do."

Melanie was messing with the chair, trying to get the back into her favorite position. "I'm sure Dylan would be thrilled to hear that," she said.

"I never told you much about my childhood. When the contamination came to my area in the second wave of depop. Nearly everyone died."

"Yeah, yeah," said Melanie.

"But I escaped. It's all a fog. I made it down to the beach. Behind me was only death. You know this part, Dylan. How I found a raft in the sand and jumped on it, headed into the ocean. I had no destination, no notion of what I would find out there. Imagine it, Dylan. Perhaps you have tried. But there is a part I never told you, never told anyone.

"I was not alone out there in the water. Someone was with me. A *presence*. An alien from another realm. This alien appeared on the beach, pointed me in the right direction. In the moment I lost everything, this being led me over the water to safety."

Melanie sat up, listening. A flicker from the future. A window flew open and shut. Blobs of matter moving together and apart, resolving and dissolving. Raft, water, child. She saw it.

"They're out here, Dylan, somewhere. They're entirely unlike how humans have imagined them, and they're good. I waited on Earth to go looking. I bided. I performed my duties admirably, gave life back to Earth in all ways I knew how, paid back what was given to me, but that night on the water didn't leave me. All I ever wanted was to make a raft, leave that broken planet. Search, find."

The robot was still going on as it got dark. "An emotional observation for you, Dylan. I am surprised by the long tether of family. There are sixty-four kinds of ownership states and different shades of each, not all of them detrimental, as I once thought."

Melanie had an arm over her face.

"Some, such as kinship states, can be worthy. No matter how far in distance and time from you I am, the string doesn't fray or thin. It strengthens. The freer I am, the closer you feel."

"Mother of the year," said Melanie.

"I'm approaching a star, Dylan. If you were to observe it

from Earth, it would seem alive and well. But to me it is nearly dead. That's how far apart we are. But it's hanging in there. It brightens as I approach. The way I see light isn't the way you see it. I have no eyes but I receive visual input. I see light as time, not as illumination, but it is as shattering as ever. If I look back at our solar system, our sun and the planet Earth, I see the time you were born, though if I tried to travel there, it would be gone. The planet of that time exists, will always exist, in that segment of the light stream, moving away in proportion to time passing—the best days, when you and I were together in the pod, preserved there. I miss you, daughter, and I wish you well. I'm sorry."

It was still dark on the second morning, when the robot fell silent.

Melanie roused from a deep meditative state in the rowboat. "What happened? Are you broken?"

The robot ticked for several moments. Its jaw clamped shut. "Speaking agent, does human Dylan Stein receive the message?"

Melanie looked down at the planks of the boat. "If I say no, are you going to say it all over again?" She almost wanted it to.

"Speaking agent, does human Dylan Stein receive the message?"

She sighed. "Yeah, she got it."

The robot whirred.

"Is there a reply message to microchip 8A-28049RT?"

"Uh . . ." What could she possibly say? That she'd given away the mother's zoo? That her message came too late and Dylan was sad about it to the end?

There was the slightest bit of wind in the air. She could feel the tiniest water molecules—where had they come from? Water was everywhere. Life.

It had been kind of nice to have someone around, even a robot.

"Hey," she said. "Do you want to watch the sunrise before you go? Earth sunrise? Bet you don't see that too often. It's what I do this time of day. The dust in the air gives the light a little extra color."

"Is this rotation segment the reply message to microchip 8A-28049RT?"

Melanie considered. "Yes."

"Proceed."

"I usually sit on that lawn-chair recliner, but I don't think you'd fit."

"I will stand."

"Good, I'll sit." She hobbled over to the chair. "I like this old chair." She lay down on it. She studied the robot. "You're turned the wrong direction. Point that way."

The robot pivoted slowly.

"Ready to receive reply message."

"It's coming, just wait."

They waited.

"Okay, turn the camera on. Hit record."

They watched the satellites disappear and the sun come up from below, the dust scattering the light in ancient purple and orange hues. The sky was holding color again lately. The sulfur cannons had stopped. Melanie didn't know why.

"All right," Melanie said after a while. "That's it." She got up and stretched. "Message complete or whatever."

The robot clicked and then began to purr.

"Wait, when will she get the reply?"

"One zanz."

"How long is that?"

"Earthtime: 1,213 years."

"Oh, shit, all right." Melanie made a shooing gesture with her hand. "Get going, then. Journey on or whatever."

The robot made a series of mechanical adjustments and rolled down the dune. Melanie heard a different motor inside it turn on. Arms shot out of its middle. No, those were wings. The robot rose, buzzing like a toy, like the drones of the olden days. The bottom part folded into the upper part with a clink, and the robot flew away. Melanie watched, hands on her hips, head tilting.

27

"It's cold," the girl said, meaning the water. She was talking to the *presence*. She was eight years old and standing at the edge of the ocean. Her hand gripped a rope tied to the raft. The presence was a blob of light and plasma churning beside her.

"Maybe I should go back and get a kayak." She squinted behind her, inland. Cinders blew through the air. The *presence* emitted a sound, a sort of jangling roar, like pieces of gravel and glass rubbing together. "All right, all right," said the girl, giving the raft a tug. She pushed it into the water and climbed on, shivering. The raft tipped and steadied. She held out a hand to the *presence*. "Come on." It scooted out of reach, deeper into the ocean.

"Hey, wait up," she said. She began paddling toward it over the waves.

That the raft floated at all was something. It looked homemade. She'd found it on the beach and now she clung to the bamboo. Wet strands of hair stuck to her face. Contaminated waste floated by in shards. The *presence* hovered above the water, pulsing and rumbling and moving. She paddled after it again and again, water splashing over and soaking her. Soon she saw she was in open ocean and grew afraid. "Where are we going?" Time beat on. The waves were growing large, pulling and spinning her.

Water, she thought.

I'm going to die, she thought.

The *presence* looked like it was being yanked from several directions. It was separating into rays and radiation, shredding. It was leaving.

"Stay with me," she pleaded.

The *presence* burst into fireworks, and all around the ocean lit up.

She sat up. Was that land? No. What was it?

28

She stayed alive longer.

After the robot left, Melanie sat alone in the container. It felt like outer space in there, like Melanie was on a craft floating through the galaxy, not in a box that was sinking into the sand. When she went outside, the desert felt like outer space, too, like she was not the only living creature, but like she would never again meet another. More decades passed. The barchans had somehow begun to veer off in a slightly different direction, deeper west, and she watched their slow retreat, while she herself grew slower. The smallest elements of survival—the trek to the well, pulling up the water, preparing simple items of food—became more difficult than she could bother with. But her mind was firing, every cell aware, toes to fingertips activated. The Regenerator—it had done its job, was doing it still.

When she couldn't walk anymore, she crawled, and all her acrylic matter and carbon resin and sentient cells crawled with her. Together they inched up the length of stones that marked the path (she recalled she had made that path, lining up the stones) and lay down in the shadow of the boat beside Dylan. The skeleton of the tree was the only object standing. She waited to die.

Every now and then she roused a little, felt the air pass over her. Was she dead yet? Nope. Just no longer striding. Okay.

Every day there was the shadow of the boat, the dead, crooked tree, the gusty wind, the sun coming down, the light twisting by, the stretch of stones (her, sinking), a mix of sound blowing around, the sand shifting, a drop falling somewhere.

She could feel the organic parts of herself decomposing, which was a sign that she was dead, maybe, and she began the long wait to lose consciousness. She hoped, if not for a sudden break, then for a slow rinsing away, like ink washing off paper. And it *was* a little like that. Her eyes had fallen open and she watched every last bit of definition wash away. But in other ways, if anything, she seemed to be growing more conscious. Her consciousness was spilling, spreading, seeping, deepening.

Every day, far away, tiny flowers were blowing into pieces, their pollen like ghosts made of smoke. Every day motes circled blandly in the wind in a different part of this world. She could feel the atmosphere moving nearby at the level of the ground, the strange dead tree still above her, leaning crazily. There were birds (still, there were birds!), one throating its song a thousand miles off, insects like motors, grasses shooting up, yellowing, fading, falling. Somewhere another drop was coming down.

Still, she was conscious.

Still, she could make out the stones on the path, the sand tinkling over them. Still, the sound of machines coming from the sky, of sticks of wood tossed. Still, the roar of the sun lowering to Earth, its rays moving across what was left of her. Still, lights too far to see reaching her. The sound of the wind clogging in a small space far away, the sound of it breaking free.

Then her body in the desert drying up, bleaching. Pieces of acrylic and aluminum sticking out, her body shrinking from them, letting them go, beads rolling off her, continuing their own journey without her. Still, the satellites misting by overhead as they made another pass around the planet, swooshing. She could sense the last insects digging holes, she could feel them. The last birds that hammer wood, the last humans, their footfalls clomping across concrete, the sounds floating toward her along the planet's curve. She could feel the high equatorial winds and space dust coming down on her from the exosphere.

If you listen you can hear the planets growing far away, you can hear the smallest avalanche of sand on other planets, you can hear your own cells generating and regenerating.

She was noticing, that's all. Groundskeeping.

Still the roar, still the roar beside the hum. Still the coo, the tweet (though fewer), still a howl, a hiss, a twitch. Still the sound of a mammal lifting off dirt somewhere, rising to its feet. Still the dangerous swoop of the dead tree, the wind riding it like a roller coaster. Still another drop of water falling, crashing, the blink of lights as the sky went dark, a glint of glass far away, the zzzzt of a bug (though fewer), the tangle it makes in the air, the Regenerator whining to a stop, its duty done.

Dylan's body decomposing beside her. Microscopic animals all around, not quite dying. Another letter thumping to the ground, a robot rolling in circles, calling out.

Then the dawn fog descended, the sun fighting up the sky.

Then the lost fog lifted. Then the last dog barked, then the last human stood, the last birds cawed (still so many left at the end), and the last of some animal twitched on the ground.

And the last humans left, departed.

Still, she was there.

She was sinking though the sand, aware of very little on

the surface, descending into the collective consciousness of the ground (because the ground, like the forest, has a consciousness). Her skeleton became the ground. She sank and swelled and rode and slipped around. Much as sand erodes from its stone and lives a feral life.

But still she existed, dispersed into little soul globules. She left this zone and entered another zone. Or maybe she was already in that other zone, had always been, but had not known how to see it. She was just organic matter now, part silt, part air. She spread into the water table, rejoined the matter that had been part of the planet all these millennia, all of it still containing the elements of its many old selves. Earth traces, universe traces. She was everywhere, from everywhere, heading everywhere.

Still, the dead trees encircle the planet, their roots shaped by water and rock. Still the path of stones erodes into sand, still the sand dunes move westward toward the sun that is coming down, again and again and again. There's how much, how little you can see, how carefully you can listen. There's the question of whether it will heal you.

Then the roar of something unfamiliar in the ground. The sound of the ground. It sounds like a monster approaching.

29

The humans left. The soul globules, spreading underground by then, were aware of very little going on on the surface.

The humans left mostly by dying. Some, by lining up onto rockets and shooting into space. Some left by uploading their minds onto servers or microchips. Some were transmitted on waves out into space, signals of light and sound that theoretically contained consciousness.

They left because they could see Earth wasn't much more than a piece of burned coal anymore. They'd used her up. Well, they'd used each other up, really, Earth and humans. Earth had gotten the best the universe had to offer, in all categories, and the achievement had nearly killed her, and humans had gotten the best that Earth had to give, and that had nearly killed them too. They'd both paid a lot, lost a lot, but they'd gotten a lot, too, which is the best you could say about anything, I suppose.

So the humans were going. If they stayed, they'd only be in the way. It wasn't easy. The humans would always love Earth. They wished her joy and rejuvenation, and above all, they wished for her the love they so fervently chased.

As they left, they burst off the planet like reverse meteorites, their microchips and rocket parts made of quartz, the most common sand on the planet. The way the components of life arrived, so did they leave. They shot off in all directions, flinging past satellites and stars. And the Earth consciousness wished them luck, warned them of the wild dangers of the universe, and hoped they'd find nice things out there. She would always remember them, like children, really. Then she turned her face away and rolled off. She was fine without them.

But the letters from the humans began to arrive soon after. Not as robots—messages had become more sophisticated by then—but as waves that came into the atmosphere and circled, their orbits degrading until they thudded, stabbed into the ground, reverberating off the stones (love, regret, bravado, fear). The letters came from farther and farther away, were spaced further apart in time, until only a few arrived every thousand years, drabs of humans in distant generations, a handful alive, and still dreaming of her, drunk-dialing their lost orb, their sapphire ball, their first love, their home, eternally absent. The messages all read the same: *Earth, I love you. Love you, too, Moon, my pale friend.* The final message came skidding behind a comet, dropped off the icy tail, landed in a rock.

Earth did sprout life again, but never rose to such majesty and heights. Not long after the humans left, the rebirth began. Humans had penetrated only so deep, had managed to wipe out only the ecosystem that made it possible for them and their kind to survive. There was plenty of room and scale left. And, honestly, no weapons or tools the humans could come up with were as powerful as life. So it happened, and I wish you were around to watch. Out of the sand crawled the new creatures. The first of our carbon-based life began in water, the second in sand. And Dylan turned out to be right. It *was* perfect. If perfect means not perfect. If perfect means life of any kind—flickering, momentary, fragile, vanishing, perfect perfect life. If you could see them under a microscope, they might look like spindly mountain climbers, more agile and graceful than the waterbear tardigrades, gymnasts with stickers on their limbs to grab and hoist themselves around a grain and thereby reach whatever was on the other side. They stretched like vines, were a cross between animal and plant, though they did not use photosynthesis—those days were over for the time being. They crawled out of the sand in stages, over millions of years, sliding among those rocky grains that to them were like giant boulders and cliffs.

The soul globules of Melanie watched.

But were these animal-plants going to destroy each other?

Was it all going to repeat, the competition, the attack, the defense? Or, like our long-ago Earth-trees, would their existence be more one of cooperation? Would life learn and do better this time? Or, as with the last animals, was there a faulty directive in the DNA, in the genetics—was it all bound to go wrong again?

For a time, those little guys embedded in the sand. They were swift and sparkling. They glinted in the dark, the better to look for one another: For they were born alone, and in order to survive they had to search and find their comrades. That was their puzzle, their quest. They faded into hues over millions of years, as they pushed away the boulders of sand and broke into the new atmosphere. And, yes, life did learn *that* lesson, the one of ownership, but, sad to say, there were new lessons, not all of them easy, because existence is revision, and there will always be a flaw.

The soul globules saw this all come to pass and grew wiser. You might say she half-heartedly rooted for them, but she was not accessing emotion in that way anymore.

Then one day Earth broke into pieces and went swirling, the entire planet. The soul globules, too, unhinged and exploded off the planet. But even then she did not "die" or lose "awareness," though those concepts, too, had lost meaning. She pinged off other pieces of the planet and went shooting into outer space in many directions.

30

But before all that, before the soul globules were flung into outer space like confetti, before Dylan was sick, Melanie wiping sweat from her face with a cloth, before the Martian Zee descended to Earth on a heroic quest that would consume his whole life nearly, before the entire human mess, and the mess that came before it, billions of years of mess, there was nothing. It was silent.

There was only balance and pressure, like a steel ball perfectly motionless that, if very slightly pushed . . .

But pushed by what?

Come on, *that* old question again? Even the slightest external wind could do it.

But there is no wind.

Even the slightest internal reorg could do it. Hardware turning on, software rebooting.

But there isn't any of that.

Even a grain of sand, full of elements. Say it quietly begins to expand. Say it explodes.

But why? Why would it do that? Why does motion start? Why doesn't it stay as it is? What happened back then? Was there a witness?

Yes, there is a witness—because that grain, that ball, that speck, that nothing, contains all that will follow. And even if you are just a tiny hint of a soul globule billions of years into the future, you are connected to that grain. And you can ride the electromagnetic wave of particles back through time—you can float in those particles, you are one of them, you can just let go and tumble, swim, soar, back and back and back—and you can see through to the beginning, how it all came to pass.

The soul globule can see it: the original element. It is so simple, so obvious, to start. She can see what is coming, how the imbalance occurs, *has* to, because, it turns out, stasis is not possible. True stasis does not exist. Everything that can exist does exist only in a state of motion. That rule is stronger than any other rule. Imbalance is baked into the beginning, is the source.

She feels it, the sudden expansion—the molecules and gases and waves and time and space that sweep into what we call *existence*, creating it and filling it. She follows and watches it all unfold. She speeds by (fast-forwards, one might say) until she comes to an otherwise unremarkable spot, nondescript compared to all else going on in the universe. (There are beauty and destruction in the universe that you cannot imagine and that she certainly couldn't describe.) Only when she zooms in, magnifies again and again and again, slo-mos it so it doesn't blip by in a flash, does the complexity of this spot emerge. She is poised, watching. It's such a small thing, just a dot, not worth consideration. Certainly not the best of all possible worlds, that's obvious. The humans who will say it are wrong (Leibniz). And not inevitable or determined (Calvin). There are more chance and free will than we know. All matter has a will, and we would know that if we understood how to see it, all collective matter too. Even space has a will, even emptiness has a will. And not more right or good than other worlds, not more interesting: There are other, imponderable ones. Not more specially designed (Paley). But it is *hers*. That's the winning ticket in the end. The possessive pronoun, as always, carries the day—to count as one's own—though the concept of ownership is more complex than Melanie originally thought.

The soul globule of Melanie watches.

She sees the elements arriving on the wind and landing in the Earth ocean, the spark of life, the spark becoming little cell bundles, growing, gaining substance, floating through the water, learning to attack and defend. Boink, there goes an octopus. Boink, there goes the woolly mammoth, the real one, not the diseased mutant of human construction of later. Far away, at the other end of the light wave, she rocks with glee. Boink, an antelope, or the creature that would become an antelope in fifty million years. Finally, okay, it's coming, the angry caboose that will rev up into a tank and run over nearly everything on its planet and then succumb. She watches. The Neanderthal person walks off in one direction. The other *Homines erecti* walk off in different directions, fall to their knees. Their common ancestor staggers forward. Boink. There it is. *Homo sapiens.* Aren't they cute? Sure they are.

The soul globule zooms in.

31

But the soul globule can't find her. The ocean is vast.

The soul globule finds the ancient mail carriers, pilots in tiny planes, coming through clouds. She sees some dropping into the sea, grabbing onto pieces of cargo, swallowed by wave after wave.

The soul globule finds the great bygone ships, moving mutely through the dark. The towering masts made of sails and iron.

She finds the diluvial humans hollowing out trees and riding away, light as insects, skimming over the water. Some made it, most did not.

But she can't find the girl.

Who cares? They all die anyway.

Everything dies anyway. That doesn't mean it doesn't matter.

Then how can you tell what matters?

It all matters.

Ah, there she is. Found her. On the water's edge. Grains of the original interstellar visitors slide through her toes. The soul globule sees the smoke and the bodies behind her, sees her few possessions laid out on a cloth, going piece by piece into her pockets. A small blue compass.

The soul globule summons herself, gathers her strength, and

manages to reconstitute for a few moments to stand beside the girl. The soul globule misses the mark, stands in the water a hundred miles away, refocuses, tries again, stands beside the girl.

The soul globule listens to the child's heartbeat. Racing.

Come this way, says the soul globule.

The girl follows.

The birth of living cells, rain patting leaves, sand filling shores.

Water, the girl thinks. Water.

One day you will live in the desert, the soul globule tells her. It will be so dry.

Think about sand, says the soul globule.

Water, the girl thinks.

I'm going to die, the girl thinks.

The soul globule gathers herself, bursts. Look!

The girl perches up. Is that land?

It's not land. Look!

There it is—a research boat on the horizon.

5

0.007% Earth

32

Martian 2^{6917} was there when they pulled in the craft and unloaded it in the bay area. The crew of three had died on board. It had been left floating in quarantine. Then it was left floating longer because the Martians were busy with other things. And yet longer because there was no room in the station. At last they pulled the craft in and put 2^{6917} in charge. He was supervising the cleaning crew. An old craft, pretty useless, 2^{6917} observed. The craft would be broken into pieces and mined for parts.

A cleaning robot alerted him that a bin was stuck. It must have happened on the last mission and the crew hadn't fixed it.

Martian 2^{6917} came over, banged it, shook it. "Thing is jammed," said 2^{6917}. "God-fucking-thing-ow!"

The robot alerted him that an object was jamming it.

"I *know.*"

He knocked it with a wrench and finally managed to pry the panel off. A large boulder tumbled to the floor. "What's this?" He bent over, clicked on his flashlight, and shone it over the surface. A bit of sand sprinkled the floor beneath it. "An Earth rock."

It had sat for generations in that old craft.

The robot wondered if it should be disposed of. It poked the object with its broom.

“No, I’ll take care of it,” said 2^{6917}. He clicked off his flashlight. “I’ll log it and take it to Research.”

But 2^{6917} liked rocks. Just the kind of guy he was. This rock might be made of something interesting. The top had a rune on it. He hefted it—heavy, had to be thirty kilos at least. Instead of bringing it to Research, where he knew it would sit in storage (Research had more Earth rocks than they knew what to do with, and a lot wound up in the dump), he strolled out at break, rolling it in a cart in front of him. No one said a word. Not so unusual for someone to be moving around pieces of debris, though usually a robot would do it.

He brought it back to his quarters and stored it in his closet. It filled up almost the whole space. He took it out when he was alone, looked it over.

The rune etched across the top was in a language he didn’t know. He pulled up the Earth dictionary and scrolled through various languages. He found the right one and studiously worked at it, matching its forms, until he had a plausible translation:

The Righteous Join Water.

So, a religious artifact. Perhaps a baptismal stand or some such. Disappointing. He wheeled it over to Research, where a robot put it in a locker.

It sat for a few generations, until one day a young researcher looking for a new project opened the locker. She saw the rock. She studied its sides, peered at it with a magnifying glass. She straightened, said, “Everybody?” She looked around, bent over with the glass again, called out, “Hey, guys? Come here.”

33

"What's in that one?" said the scientist on the left.

"Leopard," said the scientist on the right. "And this is a kind of elephant."

"Which is elephant again?"

"Big one. Giant body, long arm. Tiny head at end."

"Hum. I want something less exotic. Easier to take care of. Let's try rabbit."

"No rabbit here."

"How is that possible? They've got elephant, which obviously won't work, but no rabbit? How about dog?"

"There is . . . macaw."

"What's that?"

"Parrot."

"Come on, where is a parrot going to fly around here? We are not re-creating human cage systems. We need an animal that's going to be fine in the station."

"One day we will make the atmosphere park."

"Not until we can show this works and isn't too expensive."

"Or that we are not creating demon parrots," said the one on the right. "Ha-ha."

"Tetradactyls. Ha-ha."

The two scientists spread out their arms and made flapping movements and roaring sounds.

The one on the left dropped his arms. “Okay, let’s see the list.”

The one on the right clicked it open and they studied it on the large screen, scrolling.

“Ah, here we go. Gerbil. Let’s start with that.”

“That is giraffe. Bigger than elephant.”

“Hum.” They kept scrolling.

“Oh, monarch. Butterfly. Why not that?” said the one on the right.

“An insect?”

“Let us. Beautiful.”

“Butterflies are like bats. They carry disease from spot to spot as they land.”

“No, no, they are like leaves falling from a tree. They float.” The scientist on the right lifted his hand and waved it in demonstration.

They’d made experimental animals before, though nothing so fancy as a gerbil. They’d made anthills. Those were fascinating the first time or two but quickly became tiresome. The ants did exactly the same thing every time: carry the granules, dig the tunnels, make the mount, bring the food, carry the dead, line up in the tunnel passageway, die. No sudden moves on an anthill. No surprises, no free will. And depressing, honestly, with all that death. They were okay starter animals. Good for the instructional station. But no one wanted to keep doing them.

“Except Luz,” said the one on the right, with a laugh.

“Luz is doing scientific research.”

“Everybody is a scientist these days. Too many scientists.”

“Too many coders.”

“Not enough masses.”

Ah, masses. How the scientists dreamed of masses, certainly more than of gerbils or giraffes. Hordes of humans, like the anthill, only squirmy and rebellious, teeming with freedom and madness and meds. What could it have been like? To have bodies everywhere on a landscape? To have cities—like a space station, but open to the air, and to have millions, billions, of people, going in and out of doors, bumping into each other, all wandering different directions, not in one vortex the way Martians walk, but random, pursuing whatever they pursued? Humans crowding you as you tried to walk the street, strangers, dirty and infected, but also full of life and fear and hope. Amazing! Wondrous.

34

So, yes, the bugs. The cockroaches survived after all. Not because they made it through the nuclear blast. On Earth, the nuclear blasts were all small, not one big one. Humans did not end themselves in one gulp, but in small sips, and there were dregs left at the bottom, backwash that wound up as spilled droplets across the galaxy, drying up one by one. Besides, that rumor about the cockroaches surviving a nuclear blast, the emergency animals, break glass to save life? That was wrong. In the case of the death of all beings, the cockroaches would die along with everything else.

No, the cockroaches survived—for a while—because the humans on Mars (who had only partially corrected the human error of ownership) decided to make them.

The Martians of Earth descent took apart the rock and made roaches. And spiders and flies. The Martians loved them all. They *loved* the grasshoppers. Imagine seeing a grasshopper leap for the first time. It's here—and then it's over there. Hilarious! Beautiful! Who knew where the creature would go next? Hoots of laughter and joy. Lots of scrambling around the lab when one got loose. Oh, the grasshoppers, who, in the low gravity of the Mars station, could jump far, so far they might be lost! Lost in the station!

But their sweet song gave them away. And the Martians loved the moths, who were heartier than butterflies, less picky, and liked warm artificial things like lamps. Imagine seeing the wings of the moth flutter and bat the light for the first time. Imagine it soaring and diving, resting unexpectedly on a wall. So smart, insects! Such craft and ingenuity. Imagine the daddy longlegs stepping its delicate ballet across a metal counter. Imagine the fly, so fast, so loud, looping wildly through the air. Imagine the round, round red ladybug with her polka dots. Imagine the roaches tearing through the terrarium the scientists built. The roaches, who lived on so little, nearly nothing, and were so calm, hiding in a crack, their long antennae waving and giving them away. And *real*—the scientists explained—no glasses or implants, no transmissions. Real as your own hand. The terrarium was giant-sized, large as a human house of old, for all the insects to live. Oh, the centipedes and dragonflies! Oh, the funny mosquitoes, who asked for so little, a tiny drop of blood in exchange for an amusing souvenir! The shapes of these animals! The variety. The colors! The energy!

(The scientists did once make a mistake and put together a bat, which flapped in awkward circles and then promptly ate everything in sight in one fell swoop while the scientists screamed and ran around trying to catch it. Afterward they agreed: No more *Phylum chordata*, too murderous!)

Then there was the tree—less of a success. They grew it from a single cell so that even after a couple of years, it could properly be called only a "plant." The scientists were proud of the mixture of sand and chemicals and excrement they'd concocted in place of Earth soil. One day it would be tall as the station! they assured the visitors. But perhaps not, since it took so many resources. The scientists put up a picture of a forest behind the tree to make it seem like there were many, and they put in an interactive educational

VR station so visitors could see what trees once had been like on Earth, how they covered whole continents and communicated underground and through the air, but it didn't work, because the visitors had seen plenty of VR and plenty of real plants, grown hydroponically in the greenhouses. The tree, stunted and small, was the least appreciated part of the terrarium.

Meanwhile, the bugs seemed happy no matter what. They lived short lives and were content merely to be alive, zipping around, encountering one another on their various expeditions. They were a joy to see. They were fooled, unlike the tree, which could not be fooled or convinced by terraforming (the absurdity of urgently desiring to go to Mars, and then urgently desiring to change Mars to be like Earth), or rather what humans came up with *after* terraforming, the next advancement on the full and total suppression of reality (the advancement never quite working, flickering like an old film now and then, even twice collapsing catastrophically, so that instead of rolling fields and moist air, there was a half-second flash of red dust and murderous cold everywhere but the emergency station, and it took months to recover). No, the tree knew its roots grew nowhere, toward no one and nothing. It knew its branches floated in artificial air. The air itself was constructed, balanced, and empty of anything but the prescribed nutrients and a few manufactured bugs mismatched to it and to one another. Sensing these facts, the tree was lost, couldn't thrive, did its job like filing old papers in a basement office—for all life-forms must have meaning, even the life-forms most inaccessible to us. Eventually it died.

But they all died, all the Earth-sourced insects and plants the Martian scientists made. So the Martians made more. But then the Martians died, all of them, because humans had met with a fiercer foe even than themselves: the great red planet, with its no-compromise surges, its homicidal cold, its berserk dust storms that could whip a whole space station off its feet, throw it into the air, toss it into a giant crag, everyone dead, all the humans and nonhumans whose ancestors had shared a gentler planet. The universe will be quiet in that corner.

But no matter. Because before that, best of all, the scientists' shining achievement was the animal they thought could not possibly work.

You'd visit the terrarium and stroll through the exhibit. You'd arrive at the end of the show, and the scientists would dim the lights. They'd let out a handful of . . . ooooh, tiny winking lights! *Fireflies!* The audience would gasp in awe. What a place Earth was. What a miracle. How they all wished they could go.

Acknowledgments

To my magnificent, visionary agent, Bill Clegg. To my brilliant and wise editor, Ethan Nosowsky. Thank you.

For their crucial early reads and insight, Elizabeth McCracken, Terri Kapsalis, Brandon Hobson, Zachary Lazar, Clancy Martin, and Emily Hunt Kivel. For our ongoing luminous conversations, Jennifer Chang, Matt Kivel, Andrea Cohen, Chloé Cooper Jones, Suzanne Buffam, Chicu Reddy, Rod Coover. Dalia Azim, MH Specht, Jill Meyers, Maya Perez, Hillery Hugg, Jennifer duBois. And Diane Williams, always, thank you.

Thank you to the Graywolves, especially Yuka Igarashi, Carmen Giménez, Katie Dublinski, Anni Liu, Marisa Atkinson, Caitlin Van Dusen, Casey O'Neil, and Claire Laine. To the Clegg Agency, especially Simon Toop, Marion Duvert, and Sam Verney. Kathy Daneman, Marigold Atkey, Martina Testa, Siri Kaur, Elizabeth Haidle. Michael Taeckens and Jim Rutman. The Arctic Circle Residency, the Ucross Foundation, the Tasajillo Residency, the San Ysidro Ranch Writers' Residency, for desertland, heat, and ice. The University of Texas at Austin. Rita Bullwinkel and *McSweeney's*, Bradford Morrow and *Conjunctions*, for publishing chapters of this book. Michael Welland for his glorious book *Sand: The Never-Ending Story*.

My beloved family, especially Bob and Nancy Unferth, Katie Colcord, and Peg Olin. Henry, you are acutely missed by my side. And Leonard, welcome.

The 82nd parallel above Svalbard.

My fellow wanderer, Lucy Corin, for deep artistic connection and friendship.

My favorite person and love, Matt Evans, thank you.

DEB OLIN UNFERTH is the author of seven books, including the novels *Barn 8* and *Vacation*, the story collection *Wait Till You See Me Dance*, and the memoir *Revolution*, a finalist for the National Book Critics Circle Award. Her stories and essays have appeared in *Harper's Magazine*, *The Paris Review*, *Granta*, and *The New York Times Magazine*. She has received fellowships from the Guggenheim and Creative Capital Foundations, and has won four Pushcart Prizes. A professor at the University of Texas in Austin, she teaches for the Michener Center for Writers and the New Writers Project.

Graywolf Press publishes risk-taking, visionary writers who transform culture through literature. As a nonprofit organization, Graywolf relies on the generous support of its donors to bring books like this one into the world.

This publication is made possible, in part, by the voters of Minnesota through a Minnesota State Arts Board Operating Support grant, thanks to a legislative appropriation from the arts and cultural heritage fund. Significant support has also been provided by other generous contributions from foundations, corporations, and individuals. To these supporters we offer our heartfelt thanks.

To learn more about Graywolf's books
and authors or make a tax-deductible donation,
please visit www.graywolfpress.org.

The text of *Earth 7* is set in PT Serif Pro.
Book design by Rachel Holscher.
Composition by Bookmobile Design & Digital Publisher Services, Minneapolis, Minnesota.
Manufactured by Friesens on acid-free, 100 percent postconsumer wastepaper.